Winona: A Tale of Negro Life in the South and Southwest

Pauline Elizabeth Hopkins

WINONA
*A Tale of Negro Life
in the South and Southwest*

By
Pauline Elizabeth Hopkins
[aka Sarah A. Allen]
(1859-1930)

CHAPTER I

Crossing the Niagara river in a direct line, the Canadian shore lies not more than eight miles from Buffalo, New York, and in the early 50's small bands of Indians were still familiar figures on both the American and Canadian borders. Many strange tales of romantic happenings in this mixed community of Anglo-Saxons, Indians and Negroes might be told similar to the one I am about to relate, and the world stand aghast and try in vain to find the dividing line supposed to be a natural barrier between the whites and the dark-skinned race. No; social intercourse may be long in coming, but its advent is sure; the mischief is already done.

From 1842, the aborigines began to scatter. They gave up the last of their great reservations then before the on-sweeping Anglo-Saxon, moving toward the setting sun in the pasture lands surrounding the Black Hills.

Of those who remained many embraced Christianity; their children were sent to the pale-face schools; they themselves became tillers of the soil, adopting with their agricultural pursuits all the arts of civilized life, and cultivating the friendship of the white population about them. They, however, still clung to their tribal dress of buckskin, beads, feathers, blankets and moccasins, thereby adding picturesqueness of detail to the moving crowds that thronged the busy streets of the lively American city. Nor were all who wore the tribal dress Indians. Here and there a blue eye gleamed or a glint of gold in the long hair falling about the shoulders told of other nationalities who had linked their fortunes with the aborigines. Many white men had been adopted into the various tribes because of their superior knowledge, and who, for reasons best known to themselves, sought to conceal their identity in the safe shelter of the wigwam. Thus it was with White Eagle, who had linked his fortunes with the Senaca Indians. He had come among them when cholera was decimating their numbers at a fearful rate. He knew much of medicine. Finally, he saved the life of the powerful chief Red Eagle,

1

was adopted by the tribe, and ever after reverenced as a mighty medicine man.

Yet, through Erie County urged the Indians farther West, and took up their reservations for white settlers, their thirst for power stopped short of the curtailment of human liberty. The free air of the land of the prairies was not polluted by the foul breath of slavery. We find but one account of slaves brought into the country, and they were soon freed. But the free Negro was seen mingling with other settlers upon the streets, by their presence adding still more to the cosmopolitan character of the shifting panorama, for Buffalo was an antislavery stronghold,–the last most convenient station of the underground railroad.

It was late in the afternoon of a June day. It was uncommonly hot, the heat spoke of mid-summer, and was unusual in this country bordering upon the lakes.

On the sandy beach Indian squaws sat in the sun with their gaudy blankets wrapped about them in spite of the heat, watching the steamers upon the lakes, the constant traffic of the canal boats, their beaded wares spread temptingly upon the firm white sand to catch the fancy of the free-handed sailor or visitor. Upon the bosom of Lake Erie floated a canoe. It had been stationary at different points along the shore for more than an hour. The occupants were fishing; presently the canoe headed for an island lying close in the shadow of Grand Island, about a mile from it. The lad who handled the paddle so skilfully might have been mistaken for an Indian at first glance, for his lithe brown body lacked nothing of the suppleness and grace which constant exercise in the open air alone imparts. He wore moccasins and his dress otherwise was that of a young brave, save for feathers and paint. His flashing black eyes were fixed upon the island toward which the canoe was headed; as the sunlight gleamed upon his bare head it revealed the curly, crispy hair of a Negro.

The sunlight played, too, upon the other occupant of the canoe, as she leaned idly over the side trailing a slim brown hand through the blue water. Over her dress of gaily-embroidered dark blue broadcloth hung two long plaits of sunny hair.

Presently the canoe tossed like a chip at the base of wooded heights as it grated on the pebbly beach. The two children leaped ashore, and Judah pulled the canoe in and piled it and the paddles in the usual place, high in a thicket of balsam fir. Winona had removed her moccasins and carried them in her hand while they made the landing; Judah balanced his gun, the fishing-rods and the morning's catch of fish on a rod.

They took their way along the beach, wading pools and walking around rocks, gradually ascending the wooded heights above them round and round, until they stood upon the crest that overlooked the bay and mainland.

The island was the home of White Eagle. When the Indians gave up Buffalo Creek reservation to Ogeten in 1842, and departed from Buffalo, he had taken up his abode on this small island in the lake, with an old woman, a half-breed, for his housekeeper. Hunting, fishing, trapping and trading with the Indians at Green Bay gave him ample means of support. But it was lonely with only a half-deaf woman for a companion, and one day White Eagle brought to the four-room cottage he had erected a handsome well-educated mulattress who had escaped from slavery via the underground railroad. With her was a mite of humanity whose mother had died during the hard struggle to reach the land of Freedom. In the end White Eagle crossed the Canadian shore and married the handsome mulattress according to English law and with the sanction of the Church; the mite of black humanity he adopted and called "Judah."

In a short time after the birth of Winona, the wife sickened and died, and once more the recluse was alone. Yet not alone, for he had something to love and cling to. Winona was queen of the little island, and her faithful subjects were her father, Judah and old Nokomis.

So transparent was the air on this day in June, that one could distinguish strips of meadow and the roofs of the white Canadian houses and the sand on the edges of the water of the mainland. The white clouds chased each other over the deep blue sky. The dazzling sunshine wearied the eye with its gorgeousness, while under its languorous kiss the lake became a sapphire sea breaking into iridescent spray along the shore.

The children were on a high ridge where lay the sun-flecked woods. They were bound for the other side, where lurked the wild turkeys; and partridges and pigeons abounded, and gulls built their nests upon rocky crests.

Singing and whistling, Judah climbed the slopes, closely followed by Winona, who had resumed her moccasins. The squirrel's shrill, clear chirp was heard, the blackbirds winged the air in flight, and from the boughs above their heads the "robin's mellow music gushed." Great blossoms of pink and yellow fungus spotted the ground. Winona stopped to select from among them the luscious mushroom dear to her father's palate. Daisies and bell-shaped flowers of blue lay thick in the grasses, the maples were still unfolding their leaves; the oak was there and the hemlock with its dark-green, cone-like folliage; the graceful birch brushed the rough walnut and the stately towering pine.

The transparent shadows, the sifted light that glimmered through the trees, the deer-paths winding through the woods, the green world still in its primal existence in this forgotten spot brought back the golden period unknown to the world living now in anxiety and toil.

A distant gleam among the grasses caught the girl's quick eye. She ran swiftly over the open and threaded her sinuous way among the bushes to drop upon her knees in silent ecstacy. In an instant Judah was beside her. They pushed the leaves aside together, revealing the faint pink stems of the delicate, gauzy Indian-pipes.

"Look at them," cried Winona. "Oh, Judah, are they not beautiful?"

4

Winona

The Negro had felt a strange sense of pleasure stir his young heart as he involuntarily glanced from the flowers to the childish face before him, aglow with enthusiasm; her wide brow, about which the hair clustered in rich dark rings, the beautifully chiselled features, the olive complexion with a hint of pink like that which suffused the fragile flowers before them, all gave his physical senses pleasure to contemplate. From afar came ever the regular booming of Niagara's stupendous flood.

"But they turn black as soon as you touch them."

"Yes, I know; but we will leave them here where they may go away like spirits; Old Nokomis told me."

"Old Nokomis! She's only a silly old Indian squaw. You mustn't mind her stories."

"But old Nokomis knows; she speaks truly," persisted the girl, while a stubborn look of determination grew about her rounded chin.

"When you go to school at the convent next winter the nuns will teach you better. Then you will learn what you don't know now. You're only a little girl."

There was silence for a time; Judah sank in the tall grass and aimed for a tempting pigeon roosting low in the branches of a tree. Nearer he stole–his aim was perfect–he was sure of his prey, when a girlish voice piped,–

"Did they tell you that at school?"

"There now! You've spoilt it! why did you speak?"

"Well, I wanted to know," this in a grieved tone.

"Wanted to know what?"

"Did they tell you that at school?"

5

"Tell me what?"

"That Nokomis is silly?"

"Of course not! They didn't know old Nokomis. But in school you learn not to believe all the silly stories that we are told by the Indians."

The boy spoke with the careless freedom of pompous youth.

They moved on through the woods over the delicate tracery of shadowy foliage, and climbed down the steep sides of the hilly ridge that rose above a quiet cove on the other side where they had made what they called a kitchen. Winona led the way in her eagerness to reach the shore. She had been silent for some time, absorbed in thought.

"I tell you, Judah, I will not go to the convent school. I hate nuns."

"Ho ho!" laughed Judah. "But you must; the father has said it."

"Papa cannot make me. I will not."

"Ah, but you will when the time comes, and you will like it. I doubt not you will want to leave us altogether when you meet girls your own age, and learn their tricks."

"Stop it, Judah!" she cried, stamping her small foot like a little whirlwind, "you shall not torment me. I do not want to leave papa and you for a lot of nuns and strange girls who do not care for me."

"What, again!" said Judah, solemnly. "That makes three times since morning that you've been off like a little fury."

"I know it, Judah," replied the girl, with tears in her eyes, "but you are so tantalizing; you'd make a saint lose her temper, you know you would."

"Oh, well; we shall see–Look, Winona!" he broke off abruptly, pointing excitedly out over the bosom of the lake. Three birds floated in the deep blue ether toward the island. "Gulls!"

"No! No! They're eagles, Judah!" cried the girl, as excited as he.

"Sure enough!" exclaimed the boy.

The birds swerved, and two flew away toward the mainland. The third dropped into the branches of a maple. "It's a young eagle, Winona, and I'm going to drop him!" catching up his weapon he leaned forward, preparing to take careful aim. Suddenly there was a puff of smoke that came from behind a bend in the shore just below where they were standing. A dull report followed and the eagle leaped one stroke in the air and dropped like a shot into the waters of the lake. A boat shot out from the beach with two men in it. They picked up the dead bird and then pulled towards the spot where the children stood intently watching them. They came on rapidly, and in a moment the occupants stood on the beach before the surprised children.

They were white men, garbed in hunter's dress. They seemed surprised to see the girl and boy on an apparently uninhabited island, and one said something in a low tone to the other, and motioned toward the crisp head of the boy. They spoke pleasantly, asking the name of the island.

Winona shrank behind Judah's back, glancing shyly at them from beneath the clustering curls that hung about her face.

"This island has no name," said Judah.

"Oh, then it is not a part of the Canadian shore?"

The questioner eyes the boy curiously. Judah moved his feet uneasily in the pebbles and sand.

"'Not that I ever heard. It's just an island."

"'Do you live here?"

"Yes, over there," pointing toward the other side.

"We're mighty hungry," joined in the other man, who had pulled the boat to a safe resting place out of the reach of the incoming tide.

"We'll pay you well for your fish," he added.

"You are welcome to as much as you wish," replied Judah politely, at once passing over a number of trout and a huge salmon.

"Show them our fireplace, Judah," said Winona, at length finding her tongue. Judah led the way silently toward the sheltered cove where they had constructed a rude fireplace of rocks, and where the things necessary for their comfort during long tramps over their wooded domain, were securely hidden.

The children busied themselves with hospitable preparations for a meal, and the men flung themselves down on a bed of dry leaves and moss, lighted their pipes, and furtively watched them.

"Likely nigger," commented one.

"Worth five hundred, sure. But the girl puzzles me. What is she?" replied the one who seemed to be the leader.

"She's no puzzle to me. I'll tell you what she is—she's a nigger, too, or I'll eat my hat!" this with a resounding slap upon the thigh to emphasize his speech.

"Possible!" replied the leader, lazily watching Winona through rings of smoke. "By George! Thomson, you don't suppose we've struck it at last!"

"Mum's the word," said Thomson with an expressive wink. Judah brought some wood and Winona piled it on until a good bed of coals lay within the stone fireplace. Then she hung the fish on pieces of leather string, turning them round and round. Soon they lay in platters of birch, a savory incense filling the air, and in no time the hunters were satisfying their hunger with the delicious salmon and trout, washed down by copious draughts of pure spring water from a nearby rill whose gentle gurgle one could distinguish as it mingled with the noise of the dashing surf and the roar of the falls.

The children stood and watched them. Judah fingering lovingly the feathers of the dead eagle which he had taken from the boat.

"You haven't told us who you are," suggested the leader with a smile.

"She's White Eagle's daughter; I'm adopted."

"I see. Then you're Indians?"

Judah nodded. Somehow he felt uneasy with these men. He did not trust them.

"Not by a long sight," muttered Thomson. "Nothin' but nigger blood ever planted the wool on top of that boy's head."

Suddenly, faint and clear came a blast on a horn, winding in and out the secret recesses of the woods. Again and yet again, then all was still.

The men were startled, but the children hastily gathered up their belongings and without a word to the strangers bounded away, and were soon lost in the dark shadows of the woods.

"Well, cap't, this is a rum 'un. Now what do you reckon that means?"

"I have an idea that we've struck it rich, Thomson. Come, unless we want to stay here all night, suppose we push out for civilization?"

CHAPTER II

One sultry evening in July, about a month later than the opening of our story, a young man was travelling through the woods on the outskirts of the city of Buffalo.

The intense electric heat during the day had foretold a storm, and now it was evident that it would be upon him before he could reach shelter. The clouds sweeping over the sky had brought darkness early. The heavens looked of one uniform blackness, until the lightning, quivering behind them, showed through the magnificent masses of storm-wreck, while the artillery of the Almighty rolled threateningly in the distance.

For the sake of his horse, Maxwell would have turned back, but it was many hours since he had left the railroad, travelling by the stage route toward the city. In vain he tried to pierce the gloom; no friendly light betrayed a refuge for weary man and beast. So they went on.

Suddenly the horse swerved to one side, in affright as the electric fluid darted in a quivering, yellow line from the black clouds, lighting up the landscape, and showing the anxious rider that he was near the turnpike road which led to the main street. He spurred his horse onward to reach the road while the lightning showed the way. Scarcely was he there when the thunder crashed down in a prolonged, awful peal. The storm had commenced indeed. The startled horse reared and plunged in a way to unseat an unskilled rider, but Maxwell sat firmly in the saddle; he drew rein a moment, patted the frightened animal and spoke a few kind words to soothe his terror. On every side now the lightning darted incessantly; the thunder never ceased to roll, while the rain descended in a flood. As the lightning blazed he caught glimpses of the turbulent water of the lake, and the thunder of Niagara's falls rivalled the artillery of heaven. It is no pleasant thing to be caught by such a storm in a strange city, without a shelter.

As he rode slowly on, the road developed a smooth hardness beneath the horse's feet, the vivid flashes showed board sidewalks; they showed, too, deep puddles and sluices of water pouring at a tremendous rate through the steep, canal-like gutters which bordered the way. A disk of landscape was photographed out of the night, etching the foliage of huge, dripping trees on either side, and the wide-spreading meadows and farm lands mingled with thickets and woodland. Only a few farm houses broke the monotony of the road between the stage route and the city.

"Heavens, what a country!" muttered the rider.

It was a pleasant voice, nicely modulated, and the fitful gleams of light showed a slender, well-knit figure, a bright, handsome face, blue eyes and a mobile mouth slightly touched with down on the upper lip. A dimple in the chin told of a light and merry heart within his breast.

"What a figure I must be," he laughed gaily, thinking of his mud-bespattered garments.

With the idea of suiting his dress to the country he was about to visit, Warren Maxwell had fitted himself out in Regent street with a suit of duck and corduroy with wide, soft felt hat, the English idea, at that period, of the "proper caper" for society in America.

As he rode along the lonely way his thoughts turned with sick longing toward his English home. What would they say to see him tonight, weary, hungry and disgusted? But he had come with a purpose; he was determined to succeed. There were three others at home older than himself; his own share in the family estate would amount to an annuity scarcely enough to defray his tailor's bill. Sir John Maxwell, baronet, his father, had reluctantly consented that Warren should study law when he found that neither the church nor medicine were congenial to his youngest, favorite son. Anything was better than trade. The old aristocrat metaphorically held up his hands in horror at the bare thought. In family council, therefore, it was decided that law, with money and old family influence might

11

lead to Parliament in the future; and so Warren took up the work determined to do his best.

One day Mr. Pendleton, head of the firm, called him into his private office and told him that some one in their confidence must go to America. It was on a delicate mission relating to the heir of Carlingford of Carlingford. The other members of the firm were too old to undertake so arduous a journey; here was a chance for a young, enterprising man. If he were successful, they would be generous–in fact, he would become a full partner, sharing all the emoluments of the position at once. Of course Maxwell was interested, and asked to be given the details.

"You see," said the lawyer, "We've had the management of the estates for more than fifty years–all the old lord's time. It was a bad business when young Lord George and his brother fell in love with the same woman. It seems that Captain Henry and Miss Venton–that was the lady's name–had settled the matter to their own liking; but the lady's father favored Lord George because he was the heir and so Captain Henry was forced to see himself supplanted by his brother. Soon after a terrible quarrel that took place between the young men, Lord George was found dead, shot in the back through the heart. The Captain was arrested, tried and convicted of the crime. I remember the trial well, and that my sympathy was all with the accused. He was a bonny and gallant gentleman–the captain. Let me see–" and the old man paused a moment to collect his scattered thoughts.

"Let me see–Wait–Yes, he escaped from prison and fled to America. The lady? Why come to think of it she married a nephew of the old lord."

"And was the guilty party never found?"

"No–I think–In fact, a lot of money was spent on detectives by the old lord trying to clear his favorite and lift the stain from the family name; but to no purpose. Lord George cannot live many months longer, he is eighty-five now, but he thinks that Captain Henry may have married in America, and if so, he wants his children to inherit. For some reason he has taken a strong dislike to his nephew, who, by the way, is living in the southern part of the United States. If you go, your mission must remain a profound secret, for if he lives, Captain Henry is yet amenable to the law which condemned him. Here–read these papers; they will throw more light on the subject, and while doing that make up your mind whether or not you will go to America and institute a search for the missing man." So Maxwell started for America.

"Heavens, what a flash!" exclaimed the young man, aroused from the reverie into which he had fallen. "Ah, what is that yonder?" Before him was a large wooden house with outlying buildings standing back from the road.

"Whoever dwells there will not refuse me shelter on such a night. I will try my luck."

Urging his tired horse forward, in a moment he stood before the large rambling piazza which embraced the entire front of the establishment. From the back of the house came the barking of dogs, and as he sprang to the ground the outer door swung open, shedding forth a stream of light and disclosing a large, gray-bearded man with a good-natured face. Around the corner of the house from the direction of the outbuildings, came quickly a powerful negro.

"Well, stranger, you've took a wet night fer a hossback ride," said the man on the piazza.

"I find it so," replied Warren with a smile. "May I have shelter here until the morning?"

"Shelter!" exclaimed the man with brusque frankness, "that's what the Grand Island Hotel hangs out a shingle fer. Western or furrin's welcome here. I take it from your voice you don't belong to these parts. Come in, and 'Tavius will take yer hoss. 'Taviusl Oh, 'Tavius! Hyar! Take the gentleman's hoss. Unstrap them saddle-bags and hand 'em hyar fus'."

13

Winona

'Tavius did as he was bidden, and Warren stepped into a room which served for office, smoking-room and bar. He followed his host through the room into a long corridor and up a flight of stairs into a spacious apartment neatly though primitively furnished. Having deposited the saddle-bags, the host turned to leave the room, pausing a moment to say:

"Well, mister, my name's Ebenezer Maybee, an' I'm proprieter of this hyar hotel. What may yer name be?"

Warren handed him a visiting card which he scanned closely by the light of the tallow candle.

"'Warren Maxwell, England.' Um, um I s'pose you're an 'ristocrat. Where bound? Canidy?"

"No," replied Warren, "just travelling for pleasure."

"Oh, I see. Rich. Well, Mr. Maxwell, yer supper'll be 'bilin on the table inside a half-hour: Fried chicken, johnny cake and coffee."

In less than an hour the smoking repast was served in the hotel parlor, and having discussed this, wearied by the day's travel, Maxwell retired and speedily fell asleep.

It must have been near midnight when he was awakened by a loud rapping. What was it? Mingled with the knocking was a sound of weeping.

Jumping on to the floor, and throwing on some clothing, Maxwell went into the corridor. All was darkness; the rain still beat against the window panes now and again illuminated by sheet-lightning. Listening, he heard voices in the office or bar-room, and in that direction he started. As he drew nearer he recognized the tones of his host.

"What is it? What is the trouble?" he asked as he entered the room.

14

A strange group met his eye under the flickering light of the tallow candle–a lad in Indian garb and a girl not more than fourteen, but appearing younger, who was weeping bitterly. She had the sweetest and most innocent of faces, Warren thought, that he had ever seen. A pair of large, soft brown eyes gazed up at him piteously.

"It's White Eagle's son and daughter. Something has happened to him and they want me to go with them to the island. You see I'm a sort of justice of the peace and town constable an' I've done the Injuns in these parts some few favors and they think now I can do anything. But no man can be expected to turn out of a dry bed and brave the lake on sech a night as this. I ain't chicken-hearted myself, but I draw the line thar."

In spite of his hard words and apparent reluctance to leave home, Mr. Maybee had lighted two lanterns and was pulling on his boots preparatory for a struggle with the elements.

"Who is White Eagle?" asked Warren.

"He's a white man; a sort of chief of the few Injuns 'roun' hyar, and he lives out on a small island in the lake with a half-breed squaw and these two children. They're poor–very poor."

"What seems to be the trouble with your father?" asked Warren, turning to the stoical lad and weeping girl.

"I believe he's shot himself, sir," returned the boy respectfully, in good English. "O, come, Mr. Maybee. My father–oh, my father!" exclaimed the girl between her sobs, clinging to the landlord's hand.

The anguish of the tone, the sweet girlish presence, as well as the lad's evident anxiety under his calmness, aroused Warren's compassion.

"If you will wait a moment I will go with you. I know something of medicine, and delay may be dangerous."

Uttering a pleased cry the girl turned to him. "Oh, sir! Will you? Will you come? Do not let us lose time then–poor papa!"

"If you go I suppose I must," broke in Mr. Maybee.

"But you don't know what you're about," he continued as they left the room together: "You must remember, mister, that these people are only niggers and Injuns."

"Niggers! Mr. Maybe, what do you mean?"

"It's a fac'. The boy is a fugitive slave picked up by White Eagle in some of his tramps and adopted. The girl is a quadroon. Her mother, the chief's wife, was a fugitive too, whom he befriended and then married out of pity."

"Still they're human beings, and entitled to some consideration," replied Warren, while he muttered to himself, thinking of the tales he had heard of American slavery,–"What a country!"

"'That's so, mister, that's so; but it's precious little consideration niggers and Injuns git around' hyar an' that's a fac'."

For all his hard words, Ebenezer Maybee was a humane man and had done much for the very class he assumed to despise. He did not hesitate to use methods of the Underground railroad when he deemed it necessary.

When Warren returned to the room, the two children stood where he had left them, and as soon as Mr. Maybee joined them they started out.

Through mud and rain they made their way, the rays from the lanterns but serving to intensify the darkness. Very soon a vivid flash threw into bold relief the whiteness of the hissing lake.

"What did you come over in, Judah, canoe or boat?" shouted Mr. Maybee, who headed the party.

"The boat," called back Judah. "I thought you might come back with us."

"Good!" shouted Mr. Maybee.

When they were all seated in the boat, after some difficulty, Judah stood upright in the bow and shoved off. Each of the two men had an oar.

Not even an Indian would ordinarily trust himself to the mercy of the water on such a night, but Judah steered out boldly for the little isle without a sign of fear.

"Judah knows his business," shouted Mr. Maybee to Maxwell. "He'll take us over all right if anybody can."

At first Warren noticed nothing but the safety of the craft, and the small figure crouched in the bottom of the boat. Every swell of angry waters threatened to engulf them. The boat shivered; foam hissed like steam and spent its wrath upon them. The lightning flashed and the thunder rolled. There was no sky–nothing but inky blackness.

Rain streamed over their faces. Warren's hair hung in strings about his neck. The dangers gathered as they lessened the five miles between the mainland and the island. The young Englishman loved aquatic sports and his blood tingled with the excitement of the battle with the storm. The day had brought him adventures, but he did not shrink from death by drowning were it in good cause.

Presently the shore loomed up before them, and after much skilful paddling, they entered the sheltered cove that answered for a bay. The boat grounded and Judah sprang out, holding it fast while the others landed. It was a relief to them to feel the hard, sandy beach beneath their feet and to know that the danger was over for the present.

"Let us go faster," said Winona. "We are close now, sir–close," turning to Warren.

She ran on in front, threw open the door to the little cottage, and entered. The pictured remained with Warren always,–the bare room with unplastered floor and walls of rough boards; the rude fireplace filled with logs spouting flames; the feeble glow of the "grease lamp"; the rude chairs and tables. At one side, on a bed of skins, was extended the figure of a man. The old squaw was rocking to and fro and moaning.

"Ah! my bird!" said old Nokomis, raising her withered hands. "It is no use–it is too late."

"What do you mean. Nokomis?" demanded Winona.

"White Eagle has answered the call of the Great Spirit," replied the old woman, with a sob.

"Dead! My father!"

The girl gave one quick, heart-breaking cry, and would have fallen had not Warren caught her in his arms. Gently he raised her, and followed Judah into another room, and laid her on a bed.

"Ah," said the lad, "how will she bear it if it is true, when she gets back her senses? How shall we both bear it?"

"Come, let us see if nothing can be done for your father. Nokomis may be mistaken."

"Yes, true;" replied the boy in a hopeless tone.

Back in the kitchen where Mr. Maybee was already applying restoratives, Warren began an examination of the inanimate form before them. It was the figure of a fine, handsome man of sixty years, and well-preserved. They stripped back the hunting shirt and Warren deftly felt for the wound. As he leaned over him, he gave a startled exclamation, and rising erect ejaculated:

"This is no accident. *It is murder!*"

CHAPTER III

"Murder!"

The gruesome word seemed to ring through the silent room.

"Murder!" ejaculated old Nokomis, aghast. "It is a mistake. Who would kill White Eagle? There lives not an Indian in the whole country round who does not love him. No, No."

There was horror on the face of the young man regarding her so steadfastly. Her withered, wrinkled face was honest enough, her tones genuine.

"No!" exclaimed Mr. Maybee, recovering from the stupor into which Warren's words had thrown him. "Blame my skin! where's the blud?"

Warren regarded him steadily a moment, then said, "Look! Internal hemorrhage."

He half raised the body and pointed to a bullet hole in the back.

"By the Etarn'l!" was Maybee's horrified exclamation. "Must 'a bled to death whilst we was comin'."

Warren nodded.

"God in heaven!" cried Judah, sinking on his knees beside the bed of skins. "It is true! But who has done it? Who could be so cruel? No one lives here but ourselves. Murdered! My father! My master!"

"Hush!" said Mr. Maybee, sternly. "Hush. 'Tain't no time fer cryin' nor makin' a fuss. Tell us all you know about this business."

"He went out after supper to look after the canoes. In a short time we heard a shout and then a cry, 'Help! help!' and we ran to him,

19

Winona and I. He was leaning against a tree, and said nothing but. 'Get me to the house; get a doctor, I am hurt.' We flew to do his bidding. The rest you know."

Maxwell's brain was in a tumult of confusion. Thoughts flew rapidly through it. Suddenly he had been aroused from his solitary life in a strange land to become an actor in a local tragedy. The man lying on the bed of skins had certainly been murdered. Who then was the assassin?"

Again he looked at Nokomis, who was intently watching him. She shook her head mournfully in answer to his unasked question. Mr. Maybee was nonplussed. "What's to be done? Terrible! Murder! Why, it will kill the girl."

Warren Maxwell started. For a moment he had forgotten the delicate child in the next room rendered so suddenly an orphan, and in so fearful a fashion.

"A doctor must be summoned to certify the cause of death, and the police authorities must be notified," Warren said at length. "Right you are, pard," returned Maybee. "I'm hanged ef this business hain't knocked the spots out of yours truly. I'll take the boat and Judah here, and be back by sunrise."

He turned away, but Judah lingered, giving a wistful look into Maxwell's face.

"Yes," said Warren, laying his hand on the lad's shoulder, "I will tell her."

With a gesture of thanks Judah followed Mr. Maybee out into the night.

Pulling himself together, Warren, followed by Nokomis, entered the room where he had left Winona. She lay on the bed where he had placed her, still unconscious, her long hair lank with the rain, streamed about her face; her lips were lightly parted, even younger and more beautiful than he had at first thought; and as he remembered her story and the position that the death of her father placed her in, his soul went out to her in infinite pity.

"Poor child! Poor little thing!" he mused. "Heaven must have sent me here at this awful moment. You shall not be friendless if I can help you."

He questioned Nokomis closely. The old woman shook her head.

"Alone except for old Nokomis and Judah. White Eagle loved her very much. Old Nokomis will take care of her."

Between them the girl was restored to consciousness, and learned the truth of her father's death told by Warren as gently as possible. She heard him with a stunned expression, pale lips and strained eyes; suddenly, as she realized the meaning of his words, she uttered a piercing cry, and sprang up exclaiming:

"My father! Oh, my father! Murdered!"

She would have rushed from the room. She struggled with Warren, trying with her small fingers to unclasp his, which with tenderness held her; she turned almost fiercely upon him for staying her. The paroxysm died as quickly as it came, leaving her weak and exhausted.

Ebenezer Maybee returned at sunrise, bringing men with him. The great storm had cleared the air of the electric heat, and the morning was gloriously beautiful. The dark forest trees were rich in the sunshine, the streams and waters of the lakes laughed and rippled as happily as if no terrible storm had just passed, carrying in its trail the mystery of a foul and deadly crime. Search revealed no trace of the assassin; no clue. There were but two strangers in the city who had visited the island, and they immediately joined the searchers when they learned of the tragedy. The storm had obliterated all traces of the murderer. There was nothing missing in the humble home that held so little to tempt the cupidity of a thief. There was not even a scrap of paper found to tell who White Eagle might have been in earlier, happier days.

Everyone seemed to regard Warren Maxwell as the person in authority. The police consulted him, referred to him; Mr. Maybee confided in him, and Winona clung to him with slender brown fingers like bands of steel. As far as Warren could learn, she had no friend in the world but the hotel keeper. What a different life this poor child's must have been from any he had ever known.

Old Nokomis repeated many times a day: "Surely it was the Great Father must have sent you to us."

Judah walked about all day with a dazed expression on his face, crying silently but bitterly, and a growing look of sullen fury on his dark face that told of bitter thoughts within. Over and over again his lips unconsciously formed the words:

"I'll find him when I'm older if he's on top of the earth, and then it'll be him or me who will lie as my poor master lies in there today."

Then came the funeral. The Indians gathered from all the adjoining cities and towns and from the Canada short, to see the body of the man they had loved and respected committed to the ground. They buried him beneath the giant pine against which he was found leaning, wounded to death. Curiosity attracted many of the white inhabitants, among whom were the two strangers referred to in the first part of this narrative.

Two days after the funeral, Mr. Maybee and Warren sat in the latter's room talking of Winona and Judah.

"It was a fortunit thing for us all, Mr. Maxwell, that you happened to be aroun' during this hyar tryin' time. You've been a friend in need, sir, durn me ef you ain't."

"Yes;" replied Warren, smiling at the other's quaint speech, "it was a time that would have made any one a friend to those two helpless children."

"Maybe, maybe," returned the hotel keeper, dubiously. "But you must remember that every man warn't built with a soul in his carcass; some of 'em's only got a piece of liver whar the heart orter be." Warren smiled again.

"Mr. Maybee, I want to ask you a question–"

"Go ahead, steamboat; what's the question?"

"What is to become of Winona after I leave this place? It is different with the boy–he can manage somehow–but the girl; that is what troubles me."

"Look hyar, young feller;" said Maybee, stretching out a big, brown hand. "I don' guess she'll ever have to say she's got no friend while Ebenezer Maybee's proprietor of the grand Island Ho-tel. My wife's plum crazy to git that young kidabid. We's only awaitin' till the news of this unfortunit recurrence has blowed over, and she gits a little used to bein' without her pa. As fer Judah, thar's plenty to do roun' the stables ef he likes. But, Lor,' that lnjun-nigger! You can't tame him down to be just an' onery galoot like the most of 'em you see out hyar. White Eagle taught him to speak like a senator, ride bareback like a hull circus; he can shoot a bird on the wing and hunt and fish like all natur. Fac'." he added noting Warren's look of amusement. "Truth is,–neither of them two forlorn critters realizes what 'bein' a nigger' means; they have no idee of thar true position in this unfrien'ly world. God knows I pity em." But to Warren Maxwell it seemed almost sacrilege–the thought of that beautiful child maturing into womanhood among such uncouth surroundings. His mind revolted at the bare idea. At length he said with a sigh:

"What a pity it is that we know nothing of White Eagle's antecedents. There may be those living who would be glad to take the child."

"He was a gentleman, as your class counts 'em, Mr. Maxwell. But he never breathed a word what he was, an' he kept away from his equals—meanin' white men."

"And few men do that without a reason," replied Maxwell. "Do you know whether he was English or German?"

Mr. Maybee shook his head. "He warn't Dutch, that's certain; he was a white man all right. I cal'late he mote 'a been English."

"Mr. Maybee, I've been thinking over the matter seriously, and I have determined to write home and see if something can't be done to educate these children and make them useful members of society. In England, neither their color nor race will be against them. They will be happier there than here. Now, if I can satisfy you that my standing and character are all right, would you object to their going with me when I sail in about three months from now?"

Mr. Maybee gazed at him in open-mouthed wonder. "Yer jokin'?" he said at length, incredulously.

"No, I mean it."

Still Mr. Maybee gazed in amazement. Could it be possible that the heard aright?

"Je-rusalem! but I don't know what to say. We don' need no satisfyin' 'bout you; that's all right. But the idea of your thinkin' about edjicatin' them two Injin-niggers. You've plum got me. An' too. I cal'lated some on gittin' the gal fer my wife. Still it would be good fer the gal—durn me, but it would."

Then he turned and grasped Warren's hand hard.

"Mr. Maxwell, you're a white man. I jes' froze to you, I did the fus' night you poked yer head in the door."

"And I to you," replied Warren, as he returned the warm hand-pressure.

"Don' you ever be skeery whilst yer in Amerika an' Ebenezer Maybee's on top o' the earth. By the Etarn'l, I'll stick to you like a burr to a cotton bush, durn me ef I don't."

Again the men clasped hands to seal the bond of brotherhood.

"Meantime, Mr. Maybee, I wish you to take charge of them. I am called to Virginia on important business. I will leave a sum of money in your hands to be used for their needs while I am gone. When I return, I shall be able to tell just what I can do, and the day I shall leave for England."

Mr. Maybee promised all he asked, and then retired to the bar-room to astonish his cronies there by a recital of what the English gent proposed to do for two "friendless niggers." Maxwell rowed over to the island to tell Winona of his departure and the arrangements made for her welfare. He laughed softly to himself as he thought of his own twenty-eight years and his cool assumption of the role of Winona's guardian. Yet he was not sorry. Upon the whole, he was glad she had been surrendered to his care, that there would be no one to intrude between them; and he felt that the girl would also be glad; she appeared to rely upon him with childlike innocence and faith. How could he fail to see that the brown eyes clouded when he went away, and brightened when he approached?

He secured the boat and directed his steps to the tall pine where she usually sat now. She was sitting there by the new-made grave, her hands folded listlessly in her lap. Her eyes were fixed upon the sunlit waves and were the very home of sorrow. At that moment, turning she beheld him. A sudden radiance swept over the girl's features. Sorrow had matured her wonderfully.

"Ah! it is you. I have been waiting for you."

"You were sure I would come," he smiled, taking her hand and seating himself beside her.

"Yes. And I know you never break your word—never. You said you wished to speak to me of my future."

"Exactly. I could not go to England and leave you here alone and friendless, Winona," he replied. "I could not bear it."

The girl shivered. A month ago, she was a happy, careless child; today she had a woman's heart and endurance. Of course he must go sometime, this kind friend; what should she do then?"

"Yet I must stay. I have nowhere else to go."

"Surely you know of some friends—relatives?"

She shook her head.

"Papa never spoke of any. He used to say that we two had only each other to love, poor papa. Oh!" with a piteous burst of grief, "I wanted no one else but papa, and now he is gone."

"As He gave, so He has a right to take, Winona," said Warren, gravely. He saw that she was indeed "cast upon his care;" surely there must have been some dark shadow in White Eagle's past life to cause him to bury himself here in a wilderness among savages. Well, it must be as he had planned. He explained to Winona all that he had told Mr. Maybee.

"And you will take Judah with you?"

"Certainly," replied Warren, "You shall not be separated. The girl heaved a deep sigh of content. "I will go with you to your home gladly."

Judah was as pleased as Winona when told of the plans for the future. Each looked upon Warren Maxwell as a god. Judah went with him to the mainland. Winona saw him depart bravely. She watched the boat until they effected a landing. Once he turned and waved his hat toward the spot where she was standing. When he was no longer visible she threw herself down upon the new-made grave in an abandonment of grief, weeping passionately.

* * * * *

One month from that day Warren Maxwell, bright, smiling and filled with pleasurable anticipations drew rein again before the Grand Island Hotel. As before, 'Tavius was there to take his horse; Mr. Maybee met him at the door; but about them both was an air of restraint.

"Well, Mr. Maybee," he said gaily, "How are you, and how are my island protéges? I'll row over after dinner and surprise them."

"Come with me, Mr. Maxwell, I have something to tell you," replies his host gravely.

Surprised at his solemn manner, Warren followed him to the chamber he had occupied on the occasion of his first visit. "It's a sorry tale sir, I must tell you; and in all my life I never befo' felt ashamed of bein' an American citizen. But I can be bought cheap, sir; less than half price'll git me."

"The day after you lef' thar was a claim put in by two men who had been stoppin' roun' hyar for a month or more lo-catin thar game, the durned skunks. They was the owners of White Eagle's wife an' Judah's mother, sir—nigger traders from Missouri, sir. They puts in a claim fer the two children under the new act for the rendition of fugitive slaves jes' passed by Congress, an' they swep' the deck before we knowed it or had time to say 'scat.' Ef we'd had the least warnin', Mr. Maxwell, we'd a slipped the boy an' gal over to Canidy in no time, but you never know where a sneakin' nigger thief is goin' to hit ye, 'tain't like fightin' a man. Before we knowed it they had 'em as slick as grease an' was gone."

"But how could they take the children? They were both born free. It was an illegal proceeding," cried Warren in amazement.

"The child follows the condition of the mother. That's the law."

"My God, Mr. Maybee," exclaimed Warren as a light broke in upon his mind. "Where is she now–the poor, pretty child?"

"Down on a Missouri plantation, held as a slave!"

"My God!" Warren gazed at him for a time bereft of speech, dazed by a calamity too great for his mind to grasp. "My God! can such things be?"

(To be continued.)

CHAPTER IV

A few miles out from Kansas City, Missouri State, on a pleasant plain sloping off toward a murmuring stream, a branch of the mighty river, early in the spring of 1856, stood a rambling frame house two stories high, surrounded with piazzas, over which trailed grape-vines, clematis and Virginia creepers. The air was redolent with the scent of flowers nor needed the eye to seek far for them, for the whole front of the dwelling, and even the adjoining range of wooden stables, were rendered picturesque by rich masses of roses and honeysuckle that covered them, and the high, strong fence that enclosed four acres of cleared ground, at the end of which the buildings stood. Mingled with the scent of the roses was the fragrance of the majestic magnolia whose buds and blossoms nodded at one from every nook and unexpected quarter.

This was "Magnolia Farm," the home of Colonel Titus. He was an Englishman by birth and education who had invested his small fortune in a plantation and many slaves in the great Southwest; he had also traded in horses, selling, training, doctoring, taking care of horses, or, indeed, making money by any means that came in his way (or out of it, for the matter of that); all was grist that came to his mill. In time his enterprising spirit met with its reward and he became a leading man in all affairs pertaining to the interest of the section. The death of his wife, whom he tenderly loved, soon after the birth of their only child, had left him solitary. This affliction tendered, therefore, to deepen his interest in politics, and he eventually became one of the most bitter partisans on the side of slavery, contrary to the principles of most of his nationality. In his pro-slavery utterances he outdid the most rabid native-born Southerners. In 1854 his famous speech at St. Joseph, Missouri, at the beginning of the trouble in Kansas, had occasioned the wildest enthusiasm at the South, and the greatest consternation at the North.

"I tell you to mark every scoundrel among you who is the least tainted with abolitionism, or pro-slavery, and exterminate them. Neither giving nor taking quarter from the d—d rascals. To those

29

who have qualms of conscience as to violating laws, state or national, I say, the time has come when such impositions must be disregarded, as your rights and property are in danger. I advise you, one and all, to enter every election district in Kansas, in defiance of Reeder and his myrmidons, and vote at the point of the bowie-knife and revolver. Neither take or give quarter as the cause demands it. It is enough that the slave-holding interests wills it, from which there is no appeal."

With the memory of recent happenings in the beautiful Southland, against the Negro voter, engraved upon our hearts, these words have a too familiar sound. No, there is very little advancement in that section since 1854, viewed in the light of Gov. Davis' recent action. The South would be as great as were her fathers "if like a crab she could go backward." Reversion is the only god worshipped by the South.

Bill Thomson, whose reputation for pure, unadulterated "cussedness" was notorious in this semi-barbarous section, was his overseer and most intimate friend. Thomson's wife was the Colonel's housekeeper, and, with the owner's invalid daughter, these four persons made up the "family" of the "big house."

The summer sun hung evenly over the great fields of cotton; the rambling house cast no shadow, but the broad piazza at the back afforded ample shade from the mid-day rays, sheltered as it was by great pines; within their reach, too, lay the quarters. The porch overlooked the blooming fields where a thousand acres stretched to the very edge of the muddy Missouri. This porch, with its deep, cool shadows, commanded a view of the working force, and made it a favorite resting place for the Colonel and his daughter Lillian. The crippled girl found complete happiness seated in her rolling chair gazing out upon the dusky toilers who tilled the broad acres of foaming cotton.

His daughter's affliction was a great cross to the Colonel. His thoughts were bitter when he saw other young girls swinging along

the highway reveling in youthful strength that seemed to mock the helplessness of his own sweet girl.

"Why had this affliction been sent upon her?" he asked himself. If he had sinned why should punishment be sent upon the innocent and helpless? He rebelled against the text wherein it is taught that evil deeds shall be visited upon the progeny of the doer unto the third and fourth generations.

Far off in lovely England, ancestral halls might yet await her coming, if, perchance, Destiny should leave him in Fortune's lap. There was a letter lying snugly in his pocket, from a firm in London, that promised much, if—

It was near the noon siesta, and the Colonel sat on the piazza smoking his pipe and waiting the time to blow the horn for dinner. His daughter sat there, too, with an open book on her lap, and a dreamy look in her deep blue eyes that would wander from the printed page to the beautiful scene before her.

The sound of sharp words in a high-pitched voice and answering sobs broke in upon the quiet scene.

"There's Mrs. Thomson scolding Tennie again," observed Lillian. The words of that lady came to them distinctly from the hallway:

"What's the matter with you today? You leave your work for the other girls. What are you moping about? Is it Luke?"

"Luke been conjured," came in a stifled voice.

"By whom?"

Mrs. Thomson was a woman of considerable education and undoubted piety, but her patience was as short as piecrust. At her question all Tennie's wrath broke forth.

"Dat yaller huzzy, Clorinder; she conjured Luke till he gone plum wil' over her. Ef eber I gits my han's on her, she goin' 'member me de longes' day she lib."

"Hush, I tell you! This stuff must end right here."

"But, Mistis, dat nigger–"

"Hush your mouth! Don't you 'but' me! Do you get the cowhide and follow me to the cellar, and I'll whip you well for aggravating me as you have today. It seems as if I can never sit down to take a little comfort with the Lord, without your crossing me. The devil always puts you up to disturbing me, just when I'm trying to serve the Lord. I've no doubt I'll miss going to heaven on your account. But I'll whip you well before I leave this world, that I will. Get the cowhide and come with me. You ought to be ashamed of yourself to put me in such a passion. It's a deal harder for me than it is for you. I have to exert myself and it puts me all in a fever; while you have only to stand and take it."

The sounds died away, and once more quiet reigned. The Colonel resumed his train of thought, his brow contracted into a frown as he watched the rings of smoke curling up from the bowl of his pipe. He sighed. His daughter, watching him, echoed his sigh, because, she thought her father was changing. He was a tall, powerful man with dark hair and beard fast whitening. He had deep-set eyes that carried a shifting light; they had the trick, too, of not looking one squarely in the face.

"His hair is right gray," she said to herself, sadly, "and he is beginning to stoop; he never stooped before. He's studying, always studying about the mortgages and politics. Oh, dear, if I'd only been a boy! Maybe I could have helped him. But I'm only a girl and a cripple at that." She changed the sigh into a smile, as women learn to do, and said aloud, "Here's Winona with your julep."

The girl bore a goblet on a waiter filled with the ruby liquid and a small forest of mint. The Colonel smiled, his annoyances forgotten for a moment; he lifted the glass gallantly, saying: "Your health, my daughter!"

As he sipped and drank, the girl laughed gleefully and proceeded to refill his pipe, he watching her the while with fond eyes. Winona watched the scene with bent brows. So, happy had she been with her dead father, not so long ago.

She had passed from childhood to womanhood in two years of captivity–a womanhood blessed with glorious beauty that lent a melancholy charm to her fairness when one remembered the future before such as she. She had been allowed at lessons with her young mistress and had wonderfully improved her privileges. The Colonel and Thomson encouraged her desire for music, too; "It'll pay ten dollars for every one invested," remarked the latter. It was now two years since the two friends had returned from a mysterious absence, bringing Winona and Judah with them. The time seemed centuries long to the helpless captives, reared in the perfect freedom of Nature's woods and streams.

Winona was given to Lillian for a maid, and under her gentle rule the horrible nightmare of captivity dragged itself away peacefully if not happily.

With Judah it was different; he was made assistant overseer, because of his intelligence and his enormous strength. As graceful as vigorous, he had developed into a lion of a man. But his nature seemed changed; he had lost his sunny disposition and buoyant spirits. He was a stern, silent man, who apparently, had never known boyhood. He was invaluable as a trainer of horses, and scrupulously attentive to his other work, but in performing these duties he had witnessed scenes that rivalled in cruelty the ferocity of the savage tribes among whom he had passed his boyhood, and had experienced such personal abuse that it had driven smiles forever from his face.

Thomson wore the physique of a typical Southerner. People learning of his English ancestry were surprised and somewhat doubtful as they noted his sharp profile, thin lips, curved nose and hollow cheeks. His moustache and hair, coal black in color, increased the doubt.

As we have said, there was no greater scoundrel in Missouri than Bill Thomson. Men declared there was "a heap in him. Other bad ones were jes' onery scamps; but Bill had a head on him."

He it was who was organizing and drilling numbers of companies of men, in case the d—d Yankees proved unruly, to burn and loot the infant territory and carry it into the slave-holding lines by fire and fraud.

Into this man's hands Judah was given body and soul.

CHAPTER V

Judah's first experience of slave discipline happened in this wise: A man in Kansas City had foolishly paid five hundred dollars for a showy horse, not worth half the amount, a perfect demon whom nobody dared venture near. The purchaser was about to shoot the vicious beast, when Bill Thomson happened along, and offered five hundred even odds that he would take the animal to Magnolia Farm and break him to saddle and bridle in ten days, Thomson being of the opinion that no one knew as much about a horse or a mule as he did, and priding himself on his success with animals.

He soon found that the horse was more than he had bargained for. The beast couldn't be cajoled or coaxed–not a man daring to go near him or within reach of his head. In order to get him to the farm he was starved and drugged.

"Well, boys, I reckon it aint' no use; the ugly beast's beat me, and I lose the bet," said Thomson to the little group of men gathered at a gate of the enclosure, the next morning after the animal arrived at the farm. It was a rough group made up of gamblers and sporting men, who had heard of the bet and came to Magnolia Farm to witness the battle between the horse-dealer and horse.

"Yes, I'm licked. He's a reg'lar fiend that hoss is. I'm a done coon this day, an' the hoss will have to be shot. I invite you all to stop to the shootin' party."

"Never know'd you to git beat befo', Bill," remarked one, striking the haft of his bowie knife; "an' to lose five hundred dollars slick off, too; sho!"

"My mettle's up, boys. If I can't break the hoss in, no one can; that's true, ain't it?"

"For startin' sure!" came from the crowd.

"What's the good of lettin' a vicious brute like that live?" and Thomson ended with a volley of oaths.

"Bill's plum wil'," said one of the crowd.

"'Nough to make him, I reckon," returned the first speaker. "Bill allers did swear worse'n a steamboat cap'n. The Foul Fiend himself would be swearin' to be beat by that tearin' four-legged [beast.]

The group waited breathlessly for Thomson's next move as he stood gazing toward the refractory beast. Just at this moment Judah came up and touched his hat respectfully to the group of men.

"Don't shoot him yet, sir; I can tame that horse and win your bet for you," he said to Thomson.

It would be difficult to describe the effect produced on the group by those few cool, daring words–a breathless pause, each looking at the other in incredulous amazement; then a murmur of admiration for the speaker went from man to man, Thomson himself, who had recoiled from the boy, staring in open-eyed wonder at his cool assertion.

"You go near the beast! What do you know about breaking hosses? He'd throw you and kill you or trample you to death, an' I'd be just fifteen hundred dollars more out of pocket by the onery brute."

It was a picture for an artist,–the Negro passively waiting the verdict of his master, his massive head uncovered in humility. There was not among them all so noble a figure of a man, as he stood in a somewhat theatrical attitude–a living statue of a mighty Vulcan. Into the group Colonel Titus walked with a commanding gesture.

"Let him try, Thomson, for the honor of the farm. I believe he can do it. I'll stand the loss if there is any."

A murmur of approval broke from the crowd. At the Colonel's words, Judah stepped forward and began giving his orders without a shade of servility, seeming to forget in the excitement of the moment his position as a slave. Once more he moved as a free man amidst his fellows and for the time being forgot all else. Thomson watched him with an evil smile upon his wicked face.

"Get me a saddle and bridle ready, Sam," he called to a stable boy, "and a strong curb, too." He walked toward the stable at the end of the range which had been given up to the horse, followed by the men of the group.

"Take car', Jude," cautioned Sam. "He'll put his head out an' bite. He tried to kick de do' out yes'day!"

Heedless of the warning, Judah kept on, with the remark, "I think he's feeding."

"Take car', thar!" yelled Sam; "He's comin' at yer," as a savage snort came from within. The crowd fell back respectfully, all save Judah.

The horse rushed forwards, butting his chest against the iron bar, as he thrust his head over the top of the half-door. His ears were laid back, his eyes rolling, and his mouth open to bite, showing rows of terrible teeth. Judah did not move or tremble.

"Got grit," observed one to the other.

"Wish I owned a gang o' niggers jes' like him."

"I don't," replied his neighbor. "Them big, knowin' niggers is dang'rous."

Judah stretched out his hand and gave a half-pat to the animal's nose, withdrawing it as he attempted to seize his arm, snapping viciously.

"Stand back, all of you," commanded the boy, as he moved around, facing the animal. Then began an exhibition of mind over instinct. The power of the hypnotic eye was known and practised among all

37

the Indian tribes of the West. It accounted for their wonderfull success in subduing animals. Judah concentrated all the strength of his will in the gaze that he fixed upon the horse. Not a muscle of his powerful face moved for one instant, his glowing eyes never wavered, his eyelids did not quiver, but immovable as a statue he stood pouring the latent force on which he relied upon the vicious brute. And its effect was curious; he stared back at the boy for a few seconds with rolling eyes and grinning teeth, then his eyes wavered, he pawed the ground uneasily, flung up his head with an angry snort, half of fear, and running backwards, reared erect. Still Judah's gaze did not falter; his eyes were immovably fixed upon the uneasy animal; he dropped again, butted his muzzle on the ground, shook his mane and ran about the shed for five or ten minutes, all to no purpose; when he halted opposite the opening, Judah's unflinching gaze was still fixed upon him. A half hour must have passed in this way. At the end of that time the horse came to the opening again, trembling, and his coat foam-flecked. The men watched in breathless silence the battle-royal.

"Sugar, Sam," called Judah, still keeping his eye on the horse, and stroking his muzzle gently. The horse was much subdued, and took the lumps of sugar from his hand without an attempt at biting.

"Wal, I'm blessed!" came from the crowd.

"Hand me the bit and bridle, Sam."

"You ain't going inside, Jude?" said the Colonel.

"In a minute, yes."

With a sleight-of-hand movement a bit of sugar was in the creature's mouth, together with the bit, and the strap slipped over his head. The animal was bitted, the bridle in his conqueror's hand.

"Unbolt the door, Sam; open it wide enough for me to get in," and Judah entered the stable. "Steady, boy, steady. Sh–ho!" talking to, coaxing the half-cowed beast, the boy got the saddle on his back, and tightened the girths. "Now, gentlemen," called Judah, "Sam will fling open the door the minute I seize the bridle. Stand clear for your lives."

He gathered curb and snaffle at the loop into his bridle-hand, slid his right down and gripped it close at the bit. Before the animal could bite, rare or kick, the door was flung wide and man and steed dashed out together, Judah letting go his right hand and flinging himself into the saddle instantly, tightening the curb with both hands, and driving his feet into the stirrups.

A buzz of excitement and admiration broke from the crowd of men now too deeply stirred for words. The battle-royal had begun. The horse plunged forward, reared wildly, pawed the air, and whirled around. Judah struck him a hard blow between the ears with the whip, only to have him kick out behind in a furious attempt to throw the rider over his head. In rapid succession the animal plunged, reared, kicked, ran to and fro, and suddenly made a buckleap into the air. There was an exclamation, followed by a ringing cheer, as the men saw the boy still keeping his seat. The moment the creature's hoofs touched the ground, Judah drove the spurs into his flanks and they dashed away at a mad gallop. Then followed an exhibition of the most daring horsemanship ever witnessed in Kansas City. Rising in his stirrups, Judah, while keeping perfect control of the animal, converted the four acres of enclosure into a circus-arena, round which the horse was forced at a gallop under the sting of the whip, and in the true style of reckless Indian riding on the Western plains.

"Well done!" "Hurrah for the nigger! he's beat the hoss into the middle o' nex' week!" These and similar exclamations broke from the delighted spectators. Beaten completely, trembling in every limb and flecked with foam, the horse followed his conqueror quietly to the stables.

Colonel Titus was throwing his hat wildly up in the air in the enthusiasm of the moment, but Bill Thomson stood quietly by with an evil look distorting his face into a grin of malice and fury.

"Say, Colonel," whispered a man in the crowd, "I wudn't be in that ar nigger's shoes, not fer no money. Bill's mad 'cause he'd beat the hoss."

"Oh, that's all right. Bill's square. Come, all hands, let's go up to the house and liquor. What'll you have?" The Colonel bore the reputation of being the freest gentleman in Kansas City.

For a number of days after this affair, Thomson went about the farm in a brown study. As the men had said, he was "bilin' mad 'cause the nigger had got the dead wood on him." "He's got to be broken in; he knows too much," he might have been heard muttering between his clinched teeth.

Judah had received an ovation from the sporting fraternity and bade fair to become a popular idol. Thomson was offered large sums of money for him from several men, but refused them all with the words, "Money won't buy him till I'm through with him."

Because of his daughter's feelings slaves were never whipped on the plantation, but were sent to the slave prison in the city.

About a week later Judah was ordered to take a note to the prison in Kansas city. Being a new comer on the plantation, he was not yet familiar with its ways, and taking the note, suspecting no evil, delivered it at the "bell gate." The man who received the note after reading it called to a burly Negro: "Pete take this nigger, and strap him down upon the stretcher; get him ready for business."

"What are you going to do to me?" cried the horrified lad, at the man's words.

"You'll know d–d quick! Strip yourself; I don't wan to tear your clothes with my whip. I'm going to tear your black skin."

Finding that pleading would be in vain, the lad fought madly, until overcome by three sturdy blacks who were called in to assist. They felled him to the ground and bound him with cords.

"Take him to the shed," commanded the whipper. "String him up to a cross-beam. He's to have twenty lashes to begin with, then he's to be whipped until we have orders to stop."

Strung up by his thumbs to the cross-beams, gashed, bleeding, every blow of the whip was torturing agony. The boy uttered not a groan. He had learned his lesson of endurance in the schools of the Indian stoic, and he bore his punishment without a murmur. But every stroke of the merciless lash was engraved on his heart in bleeding stripes that called for vengeance. In the midst of the scene Thomson strolled in.

"Very good," he said, after viewing the work a moment. "Let him breathe a minute, boys, then ten more. Now, Judah, this is a taste of wholesome discipline you're getting. You've got to be brung down. I'm going to do it if I have to have you whipped every month for a year. I'm goin' to break your spirit and teach you a nigger's place; an' if your life's wurth anything to you the quicker you learn your lesson the better. No more high-head carryin', gentlemanly airs, and dictionary talk; breaking hosses in ain't wuth a cent to a nigger," he added with a malicious leer. "All right, boys, give him ten more," and while they were being administered the monster stood by calmly smoking his cigar.

"Got grit," said the whipper. "Ain't whimpered."

"Now, boys, ease up again while I finish my little speech to the gentleman."

"You've got to learn to say 'massa.' It don' matter what you can do nor how much you know, nor how handsome you think yourself, you ain't one grain better than any other nigger on the plantation. If you forget this lesson, it'll be the worse for you. Now, once more, boys," he continued, turning to the whippers, "make it a dozen and smart ones to wind up with."

* * * * *

41

Winona

All this had happened in the first year of captivity, and since that time Judah had apparently learned his place.

CHAPTER VI

It was still the pleasant month of May when, as the Colonel sat in his favorite seat on the back piazza, just before noon Bill Thomson rode up to the back of the house followed by a strange horseman.

"I've brought you a visitor, Colonel, a stranger and yet not a stranger, bein' as we've met before. He brings you news," Thomson called out as they prepared to mount the piazza steps. "Mr. Maxwell, Colonel Titus. Mr. Maxwell has come all the way from London to bring you news from the Hall. Now I know he's welcome. Mr. Maxwell sir, in the Colonel you see a Southron of the Southrons, but old England will always hold first place in his hospitable heart. So, Colonel?"

"That's the right sound, William. Mr. Maxwell, do you stop with us over night sir?"

"I fear that I must tax your hospitality to that extent. Your uncle died six months ago. The estate will be yours in one year if the direct heir is not found. Your signature will be needed to certain papers that will prove your identity and residence here, and we shall also want affidavits made out for filing. All this is a mere formality required by law. Of course, Mr. Pendleton has charge of the estates, being the family lawyer, and is only anxious that the rightful heir inherit. You remember Mr. Pendleton, do you not, Colonel Titus?"

"Oh, yes! Old Pen, we boys used to call him. I hope he'll continue to look after my affairs, if the estate comes to me. I remember him as a very reliable man."

Warren bowed in acknowledgement of the compliment paid his chief. "I have no doubt he will be pleased to serve you. There is very little doubt of your succeeding to the baronetcy–practically we have demonstrated that fact, and I think your claims pass unquestioned."

"Be seated, Mr. Maxwell; make yourself comfortable. Jude!" he called, "Jude, I say!"

Maxwell started involuntarily, as Judah came out from the hallway. At last he had found a clew to the lost ones! His pulses beat fast, but his facial muscles told no tale. But his almost imperceptible start was noticed by the two men, who exchanged glances.

"Take the gentleman's horse, and tell Mrs. Thomson we have a guest over night," said the Colonel to the waiting servant. Judah's impassive face gave forth not a gleam of intelligence as he departed to obey his master's orders.

"Now, Mr. Maxwell," said the Colonel as they sat sipping the fragrant mixture sent out to them by Mrs. Thomson by the unfortunate Tennie, "you said something about no dispute over my being next of kin. Kindly explain that remark."

"Certainly," replied Warren, smiling. "This is my second trip to America in two years, hunting up the Carlingford heirs. I thought I had found Lord George's younger son, Henry, on my first trip, but after a fruitless chase, I was forced to give it up. We are convinced that he is dead and without issue."

"Just so! Poor Henry! His was a sad fate. But it was his destiny. Do you believe in destiny, my young friend?"

"I believe that many things we call destiny may be overcome by resolving to conquer difficulties, not allowing them to conquer us."

"True, very true," replied the Colonel, meditatively.

"Mr. Maxwell, you have expressed the position of our people to a dot concerning the little difficulty we are having with Kansas. Now the North thinks they're going to beat in the fight, and the fools are going to try to fight us, but it's the destiny of the South to rule in this glorious country, an' if it ain't our destiny we'll make it so, d—d if we don't when I get the boys fixed. Got a cool two hundred and fifty coming down here from Virginia nex' week; boys who don' care a cuss what they do so long as they beat the Free States out."

"Thomson," broke in the Colonel, "it appears to me that I have seen Mr. Maxwell before. What do you say?"

"I reckon you have. Don' you remember our hunting trip at Erie two years ago? and the murder of White Eagle?"

"Sure enough! Mr. Maxwell was the young Englishman who took such a prominent part in the affair."

Warren bowed gravely.

"Most unfortunate affair! Strange, too, that the man should have been killed just when the children needed him most. If he had lived, Thomson, in all probability, would not have recovered his property." He paused with a keen glance in Warren's quiet face, but it told nothing. His voice, too, was calm and even as he inquired:

"Then Mr. Thomson was the owner of the unfortunate children?"

"Yes," returned Thomson, "I'd been hunting them gals and their mother for nigh fifteen years, an' it was just luck and chance my meeting up with them young ones."

Warren puffed away at his cigar as though it were his only object in life.

"Fine cigar," he observed, at length.

"Particularly fine. The tobacco was raised by my own hands right over there for my private use," said the Colonel.

"What do you think of our institutions, Mr. Maxwell?" asked Thomson, nonchalently. "They've made this country. 'Spose you have some compunctions of conscience over us, eh? Most Englishmen do at first. But, man, look at the advantage it gives, the prosperity it brings, the prestige it gives our fine gentry all over the world. You must confess that we are a grand people."

"Yet you complained of a tea tax, and fought a 'liberty fight' on that pretext," observed Warren drily.

"Jes' so, jes' so! But see what we've done for the Africans, given them the advantages of Christian training, and a chance to mingle, although but servants, in the best circles of the country. The niggers have decidedly the best of it. The masters suffer from their ignorance and incompetency."

"How do you think the excitement over the Kansas-Nebraska matter will end?" questioned Maxwell, avoiding a statement of his own opinions.

"There are warm times ahead. The Yankees have got to be forced to leave the States. We'll make ourselves a living terror to them. The trouble is bein' stirred up by a lot of psalm singing abolitionists and an old lunatic named Brown. Yankees won't fight; they'll scatter like chaff before my Rangers. Now, there's fighting blood for you; every man owns a nigger and loves the South and her institutions, an' they ain't goin' to be beat out o' Kansas for an extension to the institution."

"Well, gentlemen, my opinion is that you are wrong. A government cannot prosper founded on crushed and helpless humanity," replied Maxwell firmly.

"Well, well," interrupted the Colonel, "There are two sides to every question. Some day–soon, perhaps, you will realize that we are a chivalrous, gallant people, worthy of the admiration of the world."

"While the Free Staters think themselves in the right, you also feel that your side is right."

"Precisely. They have inherited their ideas as we have ours. We do not agree. It is our duty to convince them of their error, and with God's help we will do it."

"But surely, you do not defend the atrocities committed against helpless women and children that are perpetrated by your side in Kansas every day?"

"Defend them? No! But I sympathize with the feelings of the perpetrators. You condemn them wholly without comprehending them or their motives, thus injuring them and doing mischief to yourself. Each group of men in this country has its own standard of right and wrong, and we won't give our ideas up for no d—d greasy, Northern mechanic."

"That's the right sort, Colonel," nodded Thomson, in sypmathetic approval.

The announcement that dinner was served cut short further discussion, much to Warren's relief. The Colonel's words impressed the young man greatly. But ever in opposition to specious argument arose thoughts of Winona and Judah and the terrible work done at the sacking of Oswatamie.

The remainder of the day was spent in riding over the plantation, and studying the beauties of the "institution" as propounded by the philosophical Colonel. Once only, Warren's anxious gaze descried Winona wheeling the chair of her crippled mistress up and down the lawn, but when the men returned to the house both were invisible.

He and the Colonel were seated upon the piazza in the soft Southern night talking over the points of law in claiming the Carlingford estate, when Mrs. Thomson called the latter for a moment into the house. Something blacker than the black night passed him as he sat there alone. Warren was startled, and it was some moments after the figure passed, before he realized that a man had spoken to him in passing: "Leave your window unlatched."

Pleading fatigue, the young man retired early, but not to sleep. His pulse beat at fever heat; his excited fancy could detect the sound of drums and the hurrying of marching feet. He sunk into a feverish slumber, from which he was awakened by the weeping of distressed females. He listened–all was still; it was the imagination again. He could not sleep, so he arose and looked carefully after his pistols. Danger seemed all about him, but he unlatched the window and drew it back softly, then stretched himself again upon the bed.

About one o'clock he was awakened from a light slumber by some one shaking him, and sitting up, found Judah beside him,–his dark face distinctly visible by the moon's dim light. Sitting in the darkness, the sweet scent of the magnolia enveloping them in its fragrance, the faint sounds of insect life mingling with the murmur of rustling leaves. Warren Maxwell listened to whispered words that harrowed up his very soul. To emphasize his story, Judah stripped up his shirt and seizing the young white man's hand pressed it gently over the scars and seams stamped upon his back.

"I could bear it all, Mr. Maxwell," he concluded, "but Winona–" here his voice broke. "They've educated her to increase her value in the slave market, and next week Mr. Thomson takes her and me up the river to sell us to the highest bidder. If help does not come I have sworn to kill her before she shall become slavery's victim. It is impossible for me to put in words the fate of a beautiful female slave on these plantations; the torture of hell cannot surpass it."

A great wave of admiration swept over Warren at Judah's words. It was the involuntary tribute of Nature to nobility of would wherever found. The boy had become a man, and his demeanor was well calculated to inspire admiration and trust. Something truly majestic– beyond his years–had developed in his character. Warren thought him a superb man, and watched him, fascinated by his voice, his language, and his expressive gestures. Slavery had not contaminated him. His life with White Eagle had planted refinement inbred. In him was the true expression of the innate nature of the Negro when given an opportunity equal with the white man.

Impulsively, Maxwell laid his arm affectionately about the neck and shoulders of the youth.

"No extremes, Judah, until all else fails. I can buy you both if it comes to that, and my promise to take you to England with me still holds good."

"I doubt that you will be allowed to buy us. There is a stronger reason for our destruction underlying all this than is apparent. Don't let it be known that we have held any communication with you, or that you are at all interested in our fate. Be cautious."

"I will remember. But I shall have to study this matter over. I hardly know how to meet this issue if the use of money is denied us. When do you leave?"

"Monday, on the 'Crescent.'"

"Then I'll plead pressing business and leave tomorrow to meet you on board the steamer when she sails. Trust me, Judah, I will not fail you."

The tears were in Judah's throat as he tried to thank him. "I do trust you Mr. Maxwell, next to God. I knew you would be here soon; I dreamt a year ago that I saw you coming toward me out of a cloud of intense blackness. I have watched for you ever since. I was not at all surprised when I saw you riding up the avenue today; only for my hope in you as our deliverer, I'd have shot myself months ago."

"There is a God, Judah," replied Warren solemnly.

"But He seems far off from my unfortunate race," replied the man bitterly.

"Never doubt Him; His promises are aye and amen. With God's aid, I will save you or sacrifice myself."

They parted as silently as they had met.

CHAPTER VII

The steamer "Crescent" tugged and pulled at her moorings as if impatient of delay. It wanted two hours of sailing time. Down the gang-plank a strange figure sauntered, clad in buckskin breeches suspended by one strap over a flannel shirt open at the throat; high-topped boots confined the breeches at the knee; a battered hat was pushed back from a rubicand face, and about his waist a belt bristled with pistols and bowie knives. Warren smiled at the odd figure, then, with an exclamation of surprise, threw away his cigar and walked up to the newcomer.

"Mr. Maybee, of Erie?" he queried, holding out his hand.

The party addressed turned his round, smiling face in Maxwell's direction, and after one searching glance that swept his countenance in every lineament, grasped the proffered hand in a mighty clasp.

"Dog my cats, ef it ain't Mr. Maxwell! I'm pow'ful glad to meet you ag'in. How long you been here? Whar you bound?"

"I landed in New York just four weeks ago. Still on business for my firm."

"I 'spose it's in order to look out fer adventures when you an' me gits together. Remember the fus' night we met? What a swingin' ol' time we had. Poor old White Eagle! Nary sound have I heard, Mr. Maxwell, since, of them unfortoonit children neither. Might a been swallered like Jonah by the whale for all I know. I'm right chicken-hearted when I wake up at night, an' think about the leetle gal, po' pretty critter!"

"Mr. Maybee, I feel like a miserable cur whenever I think how supinely I have rested while such a horror was perpetrated–and yet I call myself a man! Your government cannot long survive under a system that thrusts free-born people into slavery as were those helpless children. May I have a word with you in private?"

Winona

"Hu–sh!" said Mr. Maybee, looking cautiously around, "them are sentimen's breathes pizen in this loorid atmosphere. Ef one of the galoots walkin' about this deck was to hear you, you'd dance on air at the yard arm in about two minutes. Them's dang'rous opinions to hold onto in free Ameriky," replied Mr. Maybee with a sly twinkle in his eye. "See that pile o' lumber out on the wharf? Well, that's the best place I know on to have a leetle private conversation with a friend. The boat won't start fer some time yet, an' I can straddle one end o' the pile an' keep a sharp lookout for listeners."

"There'll be a war in this country in less than two years, I predict," continued Maxwell, as they walked ashore. "No need o' waitin' two years, mister; jes' make it two months. The prelude to the war that's comin' was struck last fall when all Western Missouri poured into Kansas an' took the ballot out of the hands of our citizens, sir. Eli Thayer's teachin' all the North to emigrate into bleedin' Kansas an' fight it out. That's me, mister; I says to Ma' Jane, my wife, 'good-bye, Ma' Jane, ef I don't come back you'll know I've gone in a good cause, but John Brown's calling for volunteers an' I'm boun' to be in the fight.' So, I've left her power of attorney, an' the business all in her name, an' here I am. It beats all natur how fightin' jes' grows on a man once he's had a taste. Mr. Maxwell, do you know anythin' about the transfiguration of souls that some college fellars advocates? Dad gum it, I believe mos' of us must have been brutes once. Yes, sir, dogs an' vicious hosses, an' contrairy mulses an' venomous repertiles. Yes, sir, there's goin' to be a fight, an' I'm spilin' to git in it."

"Is it possible that matters are as critical as you say?"

"Critical! You may call 'em so, my boy. Six months ago I took up a claim outside o' Lawrence. One mornin', a fortnit later, twenty-eight men tied their hosses to the fence and one asked me: "Whar you from? East?' 'Yes,' says I. 'Then you're a d—d abolitionist,' another says politely. 'Of course,' says I, an' in less than a half-hour the place was cleaned out, my shack burnt to the ground an' my cattle driven off. Me an' two or three of the boys put up a decent fight or I wouldn't be sittin' here talkin' to you today. 'Taint their fault."

51

Winona

"You amaze me, Mr. Maybee."

"Do I?" queried the other with a grim smile. "Well here's another nice leetle caper o' theirs: Bud Wilson's wife writ home to her folks in Massachusetts detailin' some o' the facts concernin' the sackin' o' Oswatamie, an' addin' a few words in her own language in comments, etc., on certain actions o' the Territory militit (Missouri roughs), an' her folks let the newspapers have the whole story. My soul! The Rangers came over from this side under that devil, Bill Thomson, an' one mornin' when Bud was gone they went to the house an' took his ol' woman inter the woods an' pulled her tongue out as far as possible an' tied it to a sapling. Well, I won't pain yer feelin's by recountering the rest o' the po' critter's sufferin's, but they was the mos' dreadfulles' that you can imagine, until she mercifully gave up the ghos' and ex-pired. How's that strike you ?"

"My God!" exclaimed Warren, shuddering with horror.

"Here's another: These same Kickapoo Rangers, Bill Thomson captaing, marched to Leavenworth an' took Capt. R. P. Brown (no relation to Capt. John Brown) prisoner, he surrenderin' himself and men on certain conditions. Immejuntly the terms of that surrender was violated. One young feller was knocked down, an' a Ranger was goin' to cut him with his hatchet (Thomson has 'em all carry hatchets so as to skulp the foe like Injuns do), and Capt. Brown prevented him. After that they removed the Captaing up to Easton an' put him in a separate buildin' away from his men. Then the devils rushed on him an' beat him to the floor an' cut him in the head with their hatchets, one wound bein' many inches long an' enterin' the brain. The gallant Captaing was at the mercy of his enemies then, an' they jumped on him an' kicked him. Desparately wounded, he still lived; an' as they kicked him, he said, 'Don't abuse me; it is useless; I am dying.' Then one of the wretches–Bill himself–leaned over the posterate man an' squirted tobacco juice in his eyes. Them's our leetle ways o' doin' things in free Ameriky, Mr. Britisher, when other folks talks too free or dares to have opinions o' thar own without askin' our permission to so think contrairy agin us. Yes, sir, I'm a John Brown man. I go with Brown because I can do as I please–more

52

in-dependent-like—than as if I was with Jim Lane, 'though I'll 'low Lane's gittin' in some fine work, an' we'll swing Kansas inter line as a free State quicker'n scat when we git down to bisiness. It's these things brings me on this side noysterin' roun' lookin' for employment."

"I'm a pretty good shot, Mr. Maybee, and after I finish this matter for the firm, I should like nothing better than to put myself and my pistols at the disposal of Mr. Brown," said Warren sternly, with flashing eyes.

Mr. Maybee ejected a small stream of tobacco juice from his mouth and smoothed the end of the board he was whittling, to his entire satisfaction, before replying.

"Volunteers is ac-ceptable, certainly, ef they brings weapins and ammunition. This is goin' to be no child's play. The oppersite party is strong in cussedness; on our side, we know we're right, an' we've made up our minds to die right on the spot, but never to yield. Still, we're not advertisin' our idees on the housetops, my friend; di-plomacy, says I an' all of us, is an ef-fectooal weapin' in many cases, therefore I advocate that we perceed to di-plomate—kin' o' play 'roun a spell, an' feel the t'other side. I'll consider it an honor to nesheate you any time you feel too sot, into the ranks of the Free Soilers, John Brown, captaing. Now, what's the business you wanted to lay befo' me?"

Thoroughly aroused by Maybee's words and trembling with excitement, Warren briefly related his unexpected meeting with Judah, and the peril of the captives. Mr. Maybee listened in amazement, chewing and spitting tobacco juice like an automaton in his excitement, with many ejaculations of surprise: "Sho now!" "Want ter know!" "That ar Thomson, too! Dad gum 'im fer an onery skunk! I've jes' got to kill 'im; can't help it! He hung three of our best men down to Oscaloosa two weeks ago, tortured 'em fus' tho'." "Cu'rous how things does happen in this sinful wurl!"

"They mus' be rescued right off! right off!" he said, when Warren had finished. "We must git 'em on the Underground railroad this night. You go with the boat an' I'll cut across country an' com–moonicate with Parson Steward. We've got a good hour's start of the vessel, an' there'll be sand-bars to cross,–an',–O Lord, ef we'd only git such a thunder storm as we had the night White Eagle was murdered, it'd be the makin' of this expe–dition. It's been threat'ning all afternoon. Lord, let her come."

Briefly they arranged their plans.

"Tell Judah to git Thomson drunk; put somethin' in the liquor, if necess'ry, then git ashore somehow at Weston. I'll meet you there with hosses an' we'll put fer Steward's shack. Ef once he gits the gal in his clutches, even Bill Thomson won't git her agin."

With hurried good-byes the men separated, Mr. Maybee going up the wharf at a swift gait. Warren went aboard the steamer and seated himself in a secluded corner to watch for Judah and mature his plans.

Just before the last bell rang Thomson came aboard with his slaves. Even the rude passengers were moved by the beauty of the slave girl. Every soft curve of her waist and supple body was followed by the close-fitting cotton gown; her hair, worn short since captivity, clustered in a rich, ravelled plume about her brows and neck; the soft; gazelle-like eyes were large with anxiety, but her step was firm, and she bore herself like a young princess as she crossed the deck to go below. The girlish figure appealed to Warren's tender heart. He was used to the society of famous beauties in the proudest court of the Old World; he had flirted and danced with them in the abandonment of happy youthful hours, and more than one lovely girl had been smitten with his frank, good-looking boyish face and honest, manly bearing, but never before had his heart contracted and thrilled as it did now under the one appealing glance thrown hurriedly and timidly in his direction by the young slave girl.

Scarcely were they under way when the threatening storm was upon them. It began in a dreary drizzle with occasional mutterings of thunder.

Warren noticed that Judah was seated on the deck in the slave-pen next to an airshaft, and he concluded to find the cabin communication with the shaft and reach Judah by it.

The night fell fast. Maxwell hid himself in his stateroom before supper, having made the pleasing discovery that a port-hole in his stateroom opened directly beside Judah's seat on the deck. A note was easily slipped to the slave telling him of Mr. Maybee's plan, and asking what was the best course to pursue, then he sat there in darkness waiting a movement on Judah's part, assured that his fertile brain would find a plan of escape.

In the cabin Thomson was the center of a congenial set of kindred spirits, young Virginians, going back to St. Louis after a campaign against the Free Soilers. They were reciting the glories of the expedition,–singing, shouting and making night hideous. Their favorite song ended in an uproarious chorus:

> You Yankees tremble, and
>   Abolitionists fall:
> Our motto is, Southern Rights
>   For all!

One of their number had been fatally shot in a quarrel at a hotel in Kansas City; they were carrying the body home, and had ordered the coffin brought in and placed in the center of the cabin, where, as they said, the poor fellow might have the comfort of witnessing one more good time even though beyond the possibility of joining in it.

In the gambling and drinking bout that followed, Thomson was the most reckless, and soon he, and the rest of the party, was stretched upon the floor, on tables, and lounges in a drunken stupor from which nothing could arouse them. The few women passengers were fastened in their staterooms.

Warren took his saddle-bags in his hand, and stole out upon the deck, picking his way in disgust among the bestial party blocking his path. Half-way to Weston they had struck upon a sand-bar and there they hung, shuddering and groaning in the teeth of the storm.

He seated himself near the railing. The rolling thunder mingled with the hoarse shouting of the officers and the answering cries of the crew. There were flashes of lightning at intervals. Presently a soft touch fell on his arm. He turned and saw Judah crouching in the shadow of a mast.

"They won't be off this bar before morning. I'm going to drop a boat over the side the next heavy crash that comes. Winona is waiting just back of you. It'll take nerve, but it is the only way. We must be silent and careful."

The soft murmur ended, and once more Maxwell was alone. He had noticed the small boats standing along the sides of the vessel as he came aboard in the afternoon, but had not thought of utilizing them for the purpose of rescue. His heart heat to suffocation, his nerves were strung to their utmost tension. A soft hand stole into his; he pressed it convulsively, instinctively knowing that it was Winona, but they exchanged no words.

There came a deafening crash. The bolt struck a capstan, knocking down the first mate and glancing off into the sea. Surely God was with them. Simultaneously with the crash there was a faint plash in the water, but the vivid lightning flash that followed revealed nothing. There came a lull in the storm but confusion reigned on the vessel; no one thought of the slaves. "Now!" came a warning whisper. In an instant Warren grasped the girl about the waist, swung her clear of the railing and held her suspended by the wrists over the black, boiling flood. "All right, let her drop!" came in another whisper. Warren let go his hold and listened with bated breath for the result. There came another faint plash, a grating sound as the foaming waves carried the little craft against the wooden ribs of the steamer. Then silence.

Judah, standing uptight in the boat, caught Winona in his arms as deftly as a ball is caught and tossed from one player to another. His Indian training in managing canoes made him fearless now, and his giant strength served him well.

"All right; come ahead," came to Warren's listening ears. He dropped his saddle-bags, instantly following them; he let himself down hand over hand, then swung clear and landed lightly in the center of the frail craft, steadied by the giant black. Silently the little party rested in the shadow of the great hull until another lightning flash had passed, then each man settled an oar in the row-locks, and Judah pushed off into the night.

(To be continued.)

CHAPTER VIII

There came a knock at Preacher Sampson Steward's cabin door that same night about midnight. Instantly his mind was on the alert. He had been stretched on the bed at full length for an hour listening intently to sounds outside. The thunder and lightning had ceased, and the rain and the wind beat a monotonous tattoo against the window panes. There was a world of possibilities in that knock. He could not from the sound tell whether it heralded peace or war, and these were troublous times in Kansas. It was in Preacher Steward's nature to speak his convictions fearlessly, and this made him a special object of hatred to many pro-slavery men who would have gladly rid the country of his presence, did not his well known courage and marksmanship afford him some protection against open attack.

A tallow candle sputtered in its place on the stand. Near the stand was the window, protected by a wooden shutter. Beside him on the bed where he lay half-dressed, his wife and two children lay wrapped in slumber. The knock was repeated; Steward sprang to the floor, reached out his hand and grasped his pistols, laying them handy for use on the stand by the sputtering candle, seized his rifle, cocked it, slipped the heavy iron bolt of the door with his free hand, stepped back a pace and drew a bead on the door, then with set face and tightly drawn lips, he said firmly:

"Come in!"

The door swung open, admitting a gust of rain and wind. The tall, stout figure of Ebenezer Maybee was outlined against the blackness of the night, his attire plentifully sprinkled with the mud and rain. One hand held a driving whip, the other grasped the door-latch, while his keen eyes watched the white face behind the rifle whose muzzle almost touched his breast, yet giving no sign of fear.

"What! The parson turned fighter with a vengeance," he said at length, in quiet tones. "This ain't at all 'bligatory on you, Steward. You ought to know my knock by this time. Put up your gun."

Steward instantly complied.

"Is it you, Maybee?" he queried, standing the weapon with its muzzle against the wall. "Come in!"

"Somethin' inter-estin' you've picked up by the way of makin' your friends welcome, Steward?" Maybee replied, with a grim smile, as he closed the door and advanced to grasp the minister's extended hand.

"God forgive me, Maybee, but it is more than human nature can stand. Sunday week it was only by a special act of Providence that my congregation escaped massacre. Since then I'm a marked man. I am on special guard duty tonight."

"What's up?"

"Had a message from the Rangers."

An exchange of significant glances followed this speech.

"Oh, I see. Perhaps then we'd better bring in our fugitives at once."

"What have you this time?"

"A young man and woman and a young Englishman, who is helping them away. It's a long story. All of 'em's good shots; the gal ain't slow on a pinch."

"Good!" replied the parson, evidently relieved. "We can put her in the loft. The Lord sent you, Maybee; it's inspiration to have some one to help out in an emergency."

"You're really expectin' trouble, then?"

"Yes; but let's get them in as quickly as possible. After that I'll tell you all about it."

The storm had chilled the air, and the parson kindled a fire in the stove, throwing on a plentiful supply of wood.

"I'm ready. Come to the door."

Maybee obeyed; the parson blew out the candle, leaving the room in darkness.

"Now bring them in. I'll stay here till you return. Be careful, and lose no time."

Maybee opened the door and the darkness instantly swallowed him. When he returned with the fugitives, Steward saw dimly, by the firelight shining among the shadows, the beautiful girl and the stalwart black. He regarded Winona with a look of vague wonder and admiration. In all his life he had seen no women to compare with her.

He noted, too, the golden hair and fair complexion of the young Englishman. It was no common party that sought the shelter of his rude cabin on this stormy night. His familiar eye noted the signs of strength, too, in the youthful figures.

"Good!" he told himself. "If we do have a call from the Rangers, we'll die with our boots on; that's some satisfaction."

He beckoned to Maybee, and speaking a few words to his wife who was awake, thrust his pistols into an inner pocket, and directing Warren to bolt the door after them and not to open save at a given signal, the two men went out into the storm to feed and stable the horses. This accomplished, they returned to the house, and after carefully fastening the door, Steward lighted the candle and began preparing supper for his unexpected guests.

"Now, Maybee, where from and where bound? Tell me all about it."

Winona

In a few graphic sentences, in his peculiar mixed dialect, Mr. Maybee rehearsed the story with which we are so well acquainted.

The parson listened intently with an occasional shake of the head or a sympathetic glance in the direction of Winona. "I caught up with 'em at the ferry, an' I took the ol' road so's to lessen the chances of pur-suit or of meetin' any on-welcome company on the way. I've sent word to Captaing Brown to look out for us. It was a bluff game with odds, but we've won," he concluded.

Steward laughed.

"We have generally proved winners even with the odds against us."

Warren leaned back against the wall of the rude cabin wearied from the long nervous strain, but listening intently to all that passed.

"Judah's a lion, and Winona has the pluck of a man," Maybee went on. "She doesn't whimper, but jes' saws wood an' keeps to her instructions."

Warren spoke now.

"You have as many manœuvres to gain admittance to your house as some of the Indian fighters I used to read about when a boy. What are you expecting tonight, Mr. Steward?"

"Some of the gang," replied the parson, stopping in his occupation of cutting strips of bacon for the frying pan. "They have threatened me with vengeance because I sheltered John Brown and his men on their way north a month or two back. Reynolds brought me word this morning that they had concluded to visit me tonight. Reynolds hasn't the nerve to come out as I do, and avow his principles, but maybe it's better so that the gang don't know it; through him I keep informed of all their movements."

"Don't know thar leetle program, do you?" carelessly questioned Maybee, as he threw back the lid of the coffeepot to keep its contents from boiling over.

"No; Reynolds didn't learn that," replied Steward, as he adjusted the meat in the pan and placed it over the fire, "He thinks their intention is to decorate my anatomy with tar and feathers."

"Mos' cert'n'ly," nodded Maybee, as he took his turn at tending the frying meat while Steward sliced potatoes to brown in the bacon fat after the meat was cooked.

"Mr. Steward, if we had been of their number when we came to the door just now, what would you have done?" asked Warren.

The parson held his knife over a half-peeled potato, and looked the young man in the face, while his eyes glowed with excitement.

"Well, had you been one of Bill Thomson's riders, I would have sent a bullet through you without a word. It is written: 'This day will the Lord deliver thee into my hand; and I will smite thee, and take thy head from thee.'"

"Pardon me for what I am about to say," continued Warren, "but I cannot understand how you can reconcile such a proposed course with your profession. I make no pretention to piety myself, but I have a profound respect for those who conscientiously do."

The preacher faltered.

"Don't misunderstand me," Warren hastened to say, seeing the man of God hesitate. "I am not charging you with anything. I simply cannot reconcile the two ideas, that's all. I don't quite understand your position."

"That's jest what I've wanted to say to Steward here, many a time, but not being gifted with gab, which mos' people calls eddi-kation, I haven't been able to perceed like the prefesser," meaning our English friend, Mr. Maxwell. "Thar was that secret citizens' meetin' down in the timber, and Steward was fer shootin' down at sight without a trial all onery cusses that was even suspected of bein' onfriendly to the principles of the Free-Staters. Dad gum 'em, that's my methods to a T, but it's kin' o' rough jestice fer a parson," chuckled Maybee.

"Well, gentlemen, what would you do in my place? What show have I against a gang of ten or more men unless I meet them promptly with the initiative? What better course could I have pursued with the mob that came to our church during service? When I beheld them round about us and heard their savage cries, when I saw the terror of the women and children and bethought me of their fate if perchance, the men were all slain, I girded up my loins and taking a pistol in each hand, I led forth my elders and members against the Philistines; and I said to them: 'This day I will give the carcasses of your hosts unto the fowls of the air, and the wild beasts of the earth; that all the earth may know that there is a God in Israel.' Verily, not one was spared.

"Tonight I was here single-handed. I have a wife and two children dependent on me for support. Must I be denied the right of defense gainst superior numbers because I hate slavery and have the courage of my convictions?"

The speaker's eyes–his whole face, in fact–glowed and scintillated with holy wrath and conviction in the justice of his case.

"No, let me explain further!" Warren hastened to exclaim, "It is not your defense that I question, but your aggressive spirit. Now, as I understand it, these men are a part of the territorial militia; if so, do not your acts smack somewhat of treason?"

"Treason! the word by which traitors seek to hang those who resist them. I hate the laws that make this country a nursery for slavery, and I resist them by rescuing all who come to me for refuge. Three hundred will not excuse the number that have passed this station on the underground railroad since I have been here. Oppression is oppression, whether it enslaves men and women and makes them beasts of burden, or shuts your mouth and mine if we utter humane protests against cruelty. If this is treason, make the most of it; there's one thing certain, unless I am caught napping, they are going to pay dearly for whatever advantage they secure over me."

"I concur with you," Warren replied, rising from his seat, and pacing back and forth thoughtfully. "You have a perfect right to defend your home from brutal attack, and so long as I am here I am subject to your orders. But let us hope the storm will soon blow over; the South well see its error and the Negroes will be granted freedom by peaceful means."

Steward and Maybee laughed silently and heartily at the young man's earnest words.

"Ef you stayed 'roun' here long nuff and warn't a British subjec', my fren', you might git a taste of this scrimmage that'd con-vince you that the South is a horned hornet on the nigger question. Time 'n tide nor God A'mighty won't change the onery skunks. Them's my sentimen's."

"The storm," said Judah with wild exultation in his voice, "the storm is but gathering force. These bloody happenings which are convulsing Missouri and Kansas are but the preliminary happenings to a glorious struggle which will end in the breaking of every chain that binds human beings to servitude in this country."

Warren regarded him in astonishment.

"Why do you think so, Judah?"

"I cannot tell. But I feel that the sin will be punished in a great outpouring of blood and treasure until God says it is enough. The day of deliverance of the Negro is at hand."

"Amen! The boy is a true prophet. 'Behold, the Lord's hand is not shortened, that it cannot save; neither his ear heavy, that it cannot hear.' Bring your chairs up to the table and have some hot coffee and a bit to eat."

The meal over, from which all rose refreshed and strengthened, Steward placed a ladder against the wall and mounting it, threw back a trap door in the ceiling closely concealed by festoons of strings of dried apples and bunches of onions and herbs. He then returned to the room and lit an extra candle, beckoning Winona to follow him up the steep ascent. Speaking a few words of caution to her, he descended the ladder, which he removed and put out of sight. Warren watched his movements with great curiosity. How fast he was gaining a true knowledge of life and living here in these American wilds among a rough but kindly people. These friends of the fugitive slaves lived by but one principle, "Greater love than this hath no man."

His refined sensibilities were satisfied by the melodramatic coloring of his surroundings. The atmosphere of art had affected him enough for him to perceive the beauties of the picture made by the stalwart men, the gigantic black's refined prowess and the noble lines and graceful pose of Winona's neck and shoulders.

Preacher Steward moved out a number of wooden sea chests from beneath the tall, four-posted bed where his wife and children lay wrapped in slumber. He spread at the extreme back of the open space a pair of blankets and then signed Judah to creep under the bed; when he had done so, the parson pushed back the trunks as nearly as possible to their old positions, thus completely concealing the fugitive from view.

"We can't start before five o'clock, and we may as well get all the rest we can," said Maybee.

It was after midnight when Warren, Maybee and their host lay down upon the floor which was spread with a buffalo robe and blankets.

"It's the best the railroad can offer under the circumstances. The railroad isn't wealthy and we have to put up with some discomforts."

"This beats sleeping on the ground without blankets, as we sometimes bivouac out to Captaing Brown's camp, all holler," replied Maybee, sleepily. "Declar', I'm dead beat."

"As I understand it, this isn't a railroad; it is only hiding fugitives as they pass to Canada."

"Exactly. But many people believe in an underground railroad, with regular trains running on time, stopping points, and everything in railroad style?"

"Really?"

"You bet," grunted Maybee, half-asleep.

"Yes, sir; some men of fair intelligence, too, have faith in it. They can account for the results we accomplish in no other way. A fugitive is passed along by us, night after night, until he secures his freedom. Our methods are a profound mystery."

"Let 'm stop right thar," returned Maybee. "You fellers'd better git to sleep."

Steward extinguished the light, placed his weapons where they could be reached instantly, and laid down by Warren. The rain still fell gently down in a patter on the roof, the little clock ticked in its place over the wooden stand. Warren could not sleep. An hour passed. There was a footstep. Warren's ear alone caught the sound. He raised himself on his elbow and grasped his pistol. There were more steps. They came nearer. A hand was passed cautiously over the door. Warren touched the form of Steward.

"What is it?" he asked in a whisper.

"Listen!"

The movement at the door continued as softly as before.

"Who's there?" called out Steward.

"Travellers; we want to find the road."

"Where from?"

"Missouri."

"Where yer boun?" shouted Maybee, jumping to his feet. There was a sound of parleying in subdued voices at Maybee question. Then came the answer, "Nebraska."

"You're right for that. This is the Jim Lane route. Keep the main road and you'll not miss it," again answered Steward. A moment passed. Then came the inquiry: "Can you put us up till mornin,?"

"Cayn't do it," spoke up Maybee again. "Our beds are full. How many of you?"

"Two."

"Sorry, but you'll have to keep on. Can't do anything for you."

"Say, have you seen anything of a nigger man an' gal an' a white man a-pilotin' 'em?"

"Nary one, mister," again spoke up Maybee.

"Reckon we'll push on then."

The sound of horses' feet died in the distance.

After that there was no more sleep in the cabin, though the remainder of the night passed in quiet.

Steward and his guests were early astir. The storm had cleared. The men left the house to prepare for an early start at the first streaks of dawn; when they returned, Mrs. Steward had breakfast ready.

Silence pervaded the little band. Each was pre-occupied with thoughts he did not care to discuss.

CHAPTER IX

In the early morning light they rode away through the quiet beauty of the woods. The sweetness of the cool air was grateful to them after the feverish anxiety of the night. The dew of the morning sparkled on bud and leaf, and the sunlight sifted dimly through the trees.

Parson Steward rode at the head of the small cavalcade, and Mr. Maybee at the rear; Winona was between Warren and Judah. It was Warren, however, who had helped her to mount and who did the countless trivial things which add to one's comfort, and are so dear to a woman, coming from one man.

Winona was only sixteen, and she was dreaming the first enchanted dream of youth. She did not attempt to analyze the dazzling happiness it was to once more meet and be remembered by the one object of the pure-hearted and passionate hero-worship of her childish soul; but in which, alas! for her lay the very seed of the woman's love, that must now too surely spring up into full life, forcing her presently to know it by its right name.

For two years he had been a cherished, never forgotten memory; but whom in bodily form she was never to see again. Yet so small is the world, within a week he had suddenly walked into her life again, he had offered his frankest, loyalest friendship, and opened his prisondoors with that strong right hand of his which had both power and will.

She rode along the forest lanes in a waking dream; she was too young to look far into the future, the present was enough for her. One thing was certain, she would never, never marry, because, of course, it was quite impossible she should ever marry Warren Maxwell, and a union with another would be horrible to her.

In the life she had led as a slave, this poor child had learned things from which the doting mother guards the tender maidenhood of her treasure with rigid care; so the girl thought of marriage or its form, with the utmost freedom. No, she would try to serve this man in some way, in the course of her life, she knew not how, but sometime she would be his guardian angel—she would save his life at the sacrifice of her own—nothing was too great to render him in service for his noble generosity.

It was a child's dream in which there mingled unconsciously much of the passionate fervor of the woman, the desire to devote herself and to suffer for her hero, to die for him even, if it would serve him.

As for Warren—no man could look quite unmoved on the living picture the girl made as she sat on her horse with ease and held the reins with no uncertain hand. She was so little changed, yet so much; some taller, but the same graceful form, now so rounded, the same exquisite contour of feature, and soft, dark face so full of character, so vivid with the light of the passionate soul within.

He could not dream the wild leap and throb of the young heart as she turned and caught his blue eyes bent earnestly upon her. She had early learned control in a hard school, but the light in her eyes, the joy in her face, was beyond hiding.

That chemistry of the spirit which draws two irresistibly together, through space and against time and obstacles, kept them conscious only of each other. Winona resisted the intimation of happiness so like what had come to her in her beloved Erie's isle while with her father, yet so unlike. This joy was a beam from heaven; blessedness seemed so near.

Judah watched them, himself forgotten, and his features hardened. Was it for this he had suffered and toiled to escape from his bonds? If they had remained together in slavery, she would have been not one whit above him, but the freedom for which he had sighed had already brought its cares, its duties, its self-abnegation. He had hoped to work for her and a home in Canada; it had been the dream that had buoyed his heart with hope for weary days; the dream was shattered now. He saw that the girl would not be satisfied with his humble love.

"So it is," he told himself bitterly. "The white man has the advantage in all things. Is it worth while struggling against such forces?"

A while he mused in this strain as they swept on in silence, save for the subdued tones of the couple beside him. Then came softer thoughts, and his face lost the hard, revengeful look. He would not despair; the end was not yet. Many men had admired pretty faces. Let Maxwell beware and let it end in admiration only; he knew the worth of a white man's love for a woman of mixed blood; how it swept its scorching heat over a white young life, leaving it nothing but charred embers and burnt-out ashes. God! had he not seen. He—Judah—was her natural protector; he would be faithful to White Eagle's trust.

Towards twilight, they swerved from the direct road and entered a wooded slope. For some hours the hills surrounding Lawrence had been the point they were making. The naked woods showed the cup-like shape of the hills there–a basin from which radiated upward wooded ravines edged with ribs of rock where a few men could hold the entrance against great odds. In this basin on the edges of a creek John Brown was encamped. The smoke of a fire was visible in the dim light. As they advanced, a picket's gun echoed a warning from rock to rock. They halted then and dismounted, tying their horses to the branches of trees and stood ready to answer questions. Two men with guns came out from the bushes, with the words: "Stop thar. Free or pro-slavery? Whar you from?" Warren learned afterwards that these were two of Brown's sons.

Receiving satisfactory answers from Maybee and the Parson, our party passed on until they reached the creek where a group of horses stood saddled for a ride for life, or to hunt for Southern invaders. In an open space was a blazing fire, from which the smoke they had seen came; a pot was hung over it; a woman with an honest, sunburned face was superintending the preparations for supper. Three or four armed men were lying on red and blue blankets on the ground, and two fine-looking youths–grandsons of John Brown–stood near, leaning on their arms.

Winona

Old John Brown himself stood near the fire with his shirt sleeves rolled up, a large piece of pork in his hands which he had cut from a pig, barely cold, lying near.

In the woods' dark shadows nestled rude shelter-huts made from the branches of trees.

The travellers received a hearty welcome, and a number of women immediately surrounded Winona and hurried her to the largest hut.

Warren saw her once before leaving the next morning. "Good-bye, Winona; I shall return in a few weeks at longest. You are safe now until we can reach Canada."

"Good-bye, Mr. Maxwell. Do not speak so confidently. How can we tell that you will ever return or that I shall ever see Canada? I hate these good-byes," she said, with trembling lips.

Warren took the childish hand in his and kissed it. "Let us add 'God willing.'"

"No more time," called Parson Steward. "We've a good twenty miles and a bit before night," the next moment they had shaken hands with Maybee and Judah, and were riding out of camp.

The condition of Warren's mind was one of bewilderment. He had never in his life imagined anything like his experiences of the past few days. Now and again across the confusion of his mind, images floated vaguely–a white throat tinted by the firelight, a supple figure, a rapt young face, a head held with all a princess' grace, and dark, flashing eyes. The sound of a sweet voice, soft but not monotonous, fascinated his senses, as he recalled the tones repeating commonplace answers to commonplace questions. Somehow, the poor gown accented the girl's beauty.

Toward the close of the next day, the two men rode along in silence, save when Steward broke forth in song. He was singing now in a good baritone voice.

"A charge to keep I have,
  A god to glorify;
A never-dying soul to save,
  And fit it for the skies."

Warren listened to him dreamily. The voice chimed in harmoniously with the surroundings. The evening shadows were falling rapidly and the soft twilight folded them in its embrace. Maxwell was to stop another night at the cabin, and then riding on some fifteen miles, connect with the next boat on its regular trip to St. Louis.

Presently the singer changed his song to grand old "Coronation," his powerful voice swelling on the air-waves, mingling with the rustling of the leaves stirred by the balmy air, echoing and re-echoing through the wooded glen: "Praise God from whom all blessings flow." The young man wondered that he had never before realized the beauties of the noble hymn

All the while their horses covered the ground in gallant form. Wonderful to relate, they had met with no marauding parties; but here and there, Steward pointed out to him the signs of desolation in the dreary woods where once prosperous farms had smiled; now the winds sighed over barren fields and broken fences, and the ghostly ruins of charred houses lifted their scarred skeletons against the sky in a mute appeal for vengeance.

The horsemen came to the high-road; soon they would be out in the open, clear of the woods. Warren's mind, by one of those sudden transitions which come to us at times, seemed to carry him bodily into his peaceful English home. He could see the beautiful avenues of noble trees, and the rambling, moss-covered manse; he could see the kindly patrician face of his father, and his brothers and sisters smiled at him from every bush. The Parson was ahead.

Suddenly he saw the horse stop.

"Ssh!"

Steward threw the word of caution over his shoulder at Maxwell. They halted, standing motionless in their tracks. A moment of breathless silence passed; then came the second sound of the soft clink of metal against stone, though no one was visible in the ghostly shadows of the twilight. Warren sat motionless as Steward peered about with the stealthy caution of a fox.

Why should the horse tremble? It was a second before he realized. He lurched forward in the saddle; there was a sharp pain in his shoulder; his arm dropped useless. He heard another shot, followed by a wild shout in the "fighting parson's" voice–"Blow ye the trumpet blow!" "Slay and spare not!"

Then another shot came to his benumbed faculties; then silence; he was galloping on in the darkness. On and on his frightened horse whirled him. By this time he was so faint from his wound that he could only dimly discern objects as he was whirled past the trees. Half a mile farther, the animal stumbled as he leaped over an obstacle in the path. Riderless, he sped over the highway; Warren lay motionless under the blossoming stars.

Out from the shadows of the trees came figures and voices.

"Hold the light. He ain't dead, is he?" queried the familiar voice of Bill Thomson.

"Looks like it, but reckon he's only wounded," replied Gideon Holmes, Bill's lieutenant.

Thomson bent over the insensible man, deftly feeling his heart's motion. Then he raised himself and stood looking down thoughtfully on the youth.

It was a motley crowd of Southern desperadoes, men who stopped at nothing in the line of murder and rapine.

"Say, Jim," whispered a slight, thin man to his neighbor, "I wouldn't be in that young feller's shoes fer money—"

Winona

"What's he studyin', do ye reckon, Dan?"

"Hell!" was the expressive answer.

"What's agin the boy?" asked Jim.

"Stole two o' his niggers, so he says."

"Well, sir! Nasty mess. He won't git off easy."

"No. Say, what's Bill doin' neow? Looks interestin'."

Thomson had taken the gold from Warren's money-belt and the contents of his saddle-bags and was parcelling money and clothing impartially among his followers. Warren's revolvers were stowed in Thomson's own belt; then his garments followed suit, one man getting his boots, another his coat, still another his hat and so on.

While this was going on the unfortunate man revived and stared up into the devilish face of Bill Thomson. He groaned and closed his eyes.

"Howd'y, Mr. Maxwell? Didn't think I'd meet up with you so soon again, did you? Well, I've got you. Been after you ever since you left the 'Crescent,' and a mighty pretty chase it's been. Now, I want my niggers. I ain't foolin'. Where's they at?"

"I can't tell you," gasped Warren painfully.

"Look here, my friend, you've got to tell me. It's worth your life to you. You answer me true an' straight an' I'll make it all right for you. If you don't—" He paused ominously. "I'll let a Missouri crowd kill you! It won't be nice, easy killin', neither."

"I can't tell you," again Warren answered, looking up resolutely into the sinister face bending above him.

"Got grit," muttered Sam to Dave.

Warren was trembling, and the cold drops in the roots of his hair ran down his forehead. He was not afraid, he was a man who did not know the name of fear or cowardice, but Thomson's evil looks sent a chill to his heart. Ebenezer Maybee's words of a few nights back rang in his ears monotonously: "You might git a taste of this scrimmage that'd con-vince you that the South is a horned hornet on the nigger question."

"Well," said Bill, "made up yer mind? Spit it out!"

Warren looked him in the eye without flinching; he did not answer.

Bill Thomson was what is called "foxy." He eyed his prisoner a spell and then said in quite another tone:

"Look a-here. I ain't goin' back on old England. You're my countryman, and I'm goin' to give you a square deal. You're what we call to home a high-tined gentleman. If you'll give us all the points possible an' lead the gang by the rout you've jes' come, you needn't say one word. I don't want no man to give his pals away. Will you?"

Their eyes met. The glitter of steel crossed under the lantern's light. Maxwell compressed his lips. Winona stared at him across the shadows of the dim old woods. "Be true," she whispered to the secret ear of his soul. With rapture he read aright the hopeless passion in her eyes when he left her. He knew now that he loved her. With sudden boldness he answered his tormentor.

"You have no right to claim either Winona or Judah as your slave. They are as free as you or I. I will never aid and abet your barbarous system, understanding it as I do now."

There was a cry and a general movement on the part of the crowd.

"Let him free his mind!" said Bill, waving the men back. "What do you mean by 'barbarous system'?"

"I mean a system that makes it right to force a free man or woman into slavery. A system which makes it a crime to utter one's honest convictions."

"Wal, I reckon that'll do fer now," broke in Gideon Holmes.

"I have committed no crime against your laws; if so, why, leave me in the hands of the law."

"We take the law into our own hands these times," replied Gideon.

"Let me labor with him a spell, Gid." Gideon subsided, muttering.

"In the fus' place you are foun' guilty of associatin' with Northern abolitionists; besides that, they have so far corrupted your better judgment as to cause you to become a party to runnin' off slaves.

"Now, Mr. Maxwell, bein' a british subjec', you may not know that in the South sech actions is accountable with murder and becomes a hangin' affair. Because of your ignorance of our laws, and, whereas, you have fallen into evil company, we will give you a show for your life if you will own up and tell all you know, and help us to recover our property; otherwise, sorry as I should be to deal harshly with a gentleman of your cloth, the law mus' take its course."

"I am aware that I can expect no mercy at your hands. I have spoken freely and stated my honest convictions."

"An' free enough you've been, by gosh!" said Gideon, again breaking in.

Just at this point two men rode out of the woods leading a horse that Warren recognized. It was the parson's.

"Where's he at?" queried Bill.

"Dead's a hammer," answered the one in charge, at whose side dangled the pistols of the "fighting parson."

77

"Sure?"

"Sure."

"Git anything out of him about my niggers?"

"No use, Bill; they're up to Brown's camp. Nex' week they'll be in Canidy."

"Well, this one won't escape," said Bill, with a great oath, and a black, lowering look at the prisoner.

Without more talk, Warren was lifted to the back of the parson's horse and firmly bound. Then began a long, wild ride through the night in darkness and silence, bound, helpless, stabbed by every stumble.

Sometimes they trotted on high ground, sometimes the horses were up to their knees in the bog; and once Warren felt a heave of his horse's flanks, and heard the wash of water as if the animals were swimming. He tried to collect his thoughts; he tried to pray, but his mind would wander, and with the pain from his wound and the loss of blood, he was half-delirious. His thoughts were a jumble of hideous pictures.

Meanwhile, Sam and Dan talked together in whispers.

"Fifteen hundred dollars for the slaves or the slave-stealer, dead or alive, that's what the Colonel had advertised."

"A right smart o' money," replied Dan, "an' only eight o' us to git it."

"Kin' o' sorry 'bout the parson. It'll make again us up North," continued Sam.

"Ya-as, that's so, fur a fac'," acquiesced Dave.

"An' what a hunter he was, shoot the wink off yer eye! O, Lord, warn't he chock full o' grit. Min' the time he says to Bill, 'you ride fas', but Death'll cotch you, an' after death the judgmen'!" queried Sam.

Dan chuckled at the recollection. "Got the dead wood on Bill then, I reckon."

"You bet!" replied Sam, with emphasis.

"Dear, dear, ain't it turrible fur't have't do a man like that mean!" continued Dan.

"But 'twould be terrible to lost the money. I can't tell which would be turriblest!"

"That's a fac'."

"Who's that fool gabin'?" came in a fierce whisper from the front. Then followed silence.

They had emerged from the swamp and were riding through a high, fertile region of farming lands. The moon was rolling high in the heavens, while far toward the east was a faint lightning, the promise of dawn.

Once after crossing a bridge they pulled up and listened, and then rode off into the bushes and stood quietly in hiding. They were evidently anxious to avoid pursuit. Once pistol shots followed them as they fled through the night.

At Weston a crowd of men awaited them, and crossed over to the other side in company with Bill's party. Warren was thrown into a wagon. Presently they stepped from the boat to Missouri's shore.

CHAPTER X

Warren looked about him in the light of the flaming torches. Men poured down to the water's edge as fast as they could come. The crowds which surged through the streets day and night were rushing toward the wagon where lay the prisoner, their faces distorted like demons with evil passions.

Bill Thomson mounted the wagonseat and with an oratorical flourish recounted the prisoner's against the "principles of the institootion."

"Gentlemen, take notice!" said Gid Holmes as Bill finished. "This yere man is a abolitionist an' a nigger thief, two crimes we never overlooks, bein' dangerous to our peace and principles. What's your will, gentlemen? Speak out."

"Give him a thrashing first!" "Hang him!" "Burn him!"

And the ruffians dragged the wounded man from the wagon and threw themselves upon him–kicking him in the body–in the face and head–spitting upon him and maltreating him in every way. He defended himself well for a while; his bright head would rise from their buffeting.

"To the cross-roads!" came the hoarse cry from a thousand throats.

Tramp, tramp, on they rushed like a dark river, with cries whose horror was indescribable. It was not the voices of human beings, but more like the cries of wild animals, the screaming of enraged hyenas, the snarling of tigers, the angry, inarticulate cries of thousands of wild beasts in infuriated pursuit of their prey, yet with a something in it more sinister and blood curdling, for they were men, and added a human ferocity.

On they rushed from north, south, east and west, eyes aflame, faces distorted, the brute latent in every human being coming out from his lair to blot out the man, the awful cries, waning, waxing.

Winona

Maxwell was in the midst, half-running, half-dragged by a rope knotted about his neck. He fell; the thirsty executioners lifted him up, loosened the rope and gave him time to breath.

The tall young figure looked at the crowd with scorn. The British idea of fair play was in his mind.

"Thousands against one," he seemed to say, "Cowards!"

The crowd moved on a little more slowly, and Warren was able to keep his feet without a tremor.

Some ran on before, and began gathering wood, for it was determined to burn the prisoner as a more fearful example of the death that awaited the men who dared interfere with the "institution." Warren was dragged to the foot of the crossroads sign and securely bound; the wood was piled about him. The circle was not built as high as his knees, for a slow fire steadily increased, would prolong the enjoyment. Thomson himself carried the brand to light the pile. His eyes met Warren's as he knelt with the blazing pine. Not a word passed between them. A horrible and engrossing interest kept every eve on the glowing light. Presently the barrier of flame began to rise. A thousand voiced cry of brutal triumph arose– not to the skies, so vile a thing could never find the heavenly blue; it must have fallen to the regions of the lost.

They who speak or think lightly of a mob have never heard its voice nor seen its horrible work.

(To be continued.)

CHAPTER X.–(Concluded)

From the town came the ringing of bells set in motion when the party landed, still startling the night with their brazen clamor. The wildest excitement prevailed—armed riders dashed recklessly up and down in front of the place of execution, yelling, cursing, threatening.

The most trivial incidents accompany the progress of death. Warren noticed the faint light of the morning chasing away the stars. His keen sight lost not one change in the landscape. Children were in the crowd worming their way among the promiscuous legs and arms in the endeavor to gain a peep at the proceedings; one wee tot had fallen over backwards felled by the unexpected movement of the particular legs that obstructed his view. Warren was conscious of a deep sense of pity for the infants whom ignorance tortured from childhood's simple holiness as cruelly as the mob was about to torture him. There came to him then a realizing sense of all the Immortal Son must have suffered on His way to Golgotha to die a shameful death through the ignorance and cruelty of a heartless world. If the story of the crucifixion had at times presented difficuties to an inquiring, analytical mind, this experience cleared away the shadows and the application of the story of the Redeemer came to him as a live coal from the altar of Infinite Truth.

The crew of the ferry-boat was hurrying forward with the wood stored aboard for the fires under the boilers; sounds of chopping came to his ears above the yells and shouts of the mob, and reverberated along the edges of the sky. Men were chopping fuel, others ran with arm-loads of it to build around the stake which had the festive air of a May-pole. Another group thought that the spectacle needed illumination at its beginning and were heaping fuel on a camp-fire, and its crackle could be heard almost as far as its light reached.

Men swaggered about the vast bluster and deep curses, howling for the sacrifice, quenching their thirst and fanning their fury anew at a temporary bar in the wagon where an enterprising individual was dispensing drinks to the crowd at a nominal price.

The sky overhead began to assume a roseate tinge. Swarming figures became more and more distinct. The fragrant wind encroaching from the woods, bringing its sweet odors, swept the smoke sidewise like an inverted curtain.

All was ready. There came a deafening cheer when Thomson moved pompously forward and with a theatrical gesture applied the torch; then followed silence deep and breathless as they waited to gloat over the victim's first awful shriek of agony.

The flames rose. Warren ground his teeth, determined to die and make no moan to please and gratify the crowd. The sweat of physical anguish and faintness moved in drops on his forehead. His face was distinctly visible in the fierce glare. His arms were bound down against his sides, the wounded one causing him frightful torture. His shirt was open at the throat, showing the ivory firmness of his chest and the beating pulse in the white brawn. As the flames gathered headway the sky grew brighter and the shadows melted away; the crowing of cocks came faintly, above the horrid din, borne on the young morning air.

Suddenly off to the right came the sound of galloping hoofs. So imperative was the clatter that the attention of the crowd was forced for a moment from the victim at the stake.

On, on swept the riders in mad haste to the scene of torture, now distinctly visible through the cloud of dust that had at first partially concealed them from view; and now they rose in their stirrups shouting and waving their hats as if in warning. The fiends about the funeral pile made way for the cavalcade which was headed by Colonel Titus. All the party wore the uniform of State constables. "Halt!" cried the Colonel as he sprang from his horse at the edge of the crowd and cleared the open space immediately in front of the signpost at one bound, followed by his companions. The crowd fell back respectfully. He and his men kicked the blazing wood from the stake, and scattered it with hands and feet as far as they could throw it. His own clothing smoked, and his face flamed with the exertion The colonel cut Warren's bonds, while his men continued to stamp out the fire. The crowd watched them in sullen silence.

"Fools!" he shouted, when at length the fire's headway was subdued, "what are you doing?"

"Burning a nigger-thief," shouted Gideon Holmes in reply.

"None of your monkeyin', Bill Thomson; speak up. You had charge of this affair," said Titus, not deigning to notice Holmes. Bill answered with a vile oath.

The crowd stood about in curious clusters. As the fire died down, the dawn became more pronounced. The brutal carnival seemed about to die out with the darkness as quickly as it had arisen.

"And you have been allowing your men to do that which will put us in the power of every Northern mudsill of an abolitionist, and eventually turn the tide which is now in our favor, against us!" The Colonel wheeled about and faced Thomson. "Was this the understanding when you started on the expedition?"

Bill still stood sullen-faced and silent before his accuser.

"Have we not jails strong enough to hold prisoners?" Titus asked, significantly.

"Dead men tell no tales," declared Thomson, with a long look into his questioner's eyes.

"True," returned the Colonel with an answering glance. "But let all things be done in decency and order and according to the process of law. This man ain't no army. There warn't no need of your raisin' and chasin' and burnin' him like a parcel of idiots."

Winona

"'Pears to me you're d— finicky 'bout law an' all that jes' this particular time," sneered Bill, with an evil leer on his face.

The Colonel eyed him keenly while a look of disgust spread slowly over his speaking face.

"Thomson, I gave you credit for having more sense. This man is a British subject. How are we to impress the world with our fair and impartial dealing with all mankind, and the slavery question in particular, if you and a lot more hotheaded galoots go to work and call us liars by breaking the slate?"

There were murmurs of approval from the crowd.

"Fac' is thar's nothin' fer us to do but to light out, ain't that the idee, Colonel?" asked Jim Murphy.

"That's the idea, Murphy; burn the wind the whole caboodle of you!" The crowd began to disperse slowly.

"All very good," broke in Thomson with a swagger. "I'll take mine without the law. I'd ruther stay right here and carry out the programme, it'd be more satisfactory to the boys in the long run. Law is a delusion, as the poet says, an' a snare. We git plenty o' law an' no jestice. S'pose the law lets the prisoner go free? You'll be a real pop'lar candidate fer Missouri's next gov'ner."

"No fear of that in this State," replied the Colonel with an ugly, brutal look that caused a shudder to creep over Warren who was surrounded by the constables. So full of malice were the tone and look that all signs of the polished elderly gentleman and doting father were lost, and one felt that this man could perpetrate any crime, however foul. In spite of the quiet tones the Colonel's blood was at boiling point because of Thomson's stubborness. Titus turned to the constables: "Gentlemen, secure the prisoner. Thomson, fall in there and lend a hand; be quick about it. We've had too much of your fool talk a'ready. When I give my men an order, I 'low for them to obey me right up to the chalk mark."

85

Bill gave him a long look and without a word mounted his horse, and rode away–not with the troop.

The constables instantly obeyed the Colonel's order, and in a second Warren was lifted to the floor of the wagon and driven rapidly toward the jail.

CHAPTER XI

In the Brown camp the great family of fugitives dwelt together in guileless and trusting brotherhood under the patriarchal care of Captain Brown, who daily praised the Eternal Sire, and one soul of harmony and love was infused into each individual dweller.

John Brown was a man of deep religious convictions; but mingled with austerity were perfect gentleness and self-renunciation which inspired love in every breast. But amid the self-denying calmness of his deportment, those who looked deeply into his eyes might discern some cast of that quiet and determined courage which faced his enemies in later years before the Virginia tribunal where, threatened with an ignominious death, he made the unmoved reply–"I am about God's work; He will take care of me."

The fugitive slaves who came in fear and trembling were strengthened and improved by contact with the free, strong spirit of their rescuer and his associate helpers of proscribed Free Staters.

Weeks must elapse, perhaps, before a force of sufficient strength could be organized to protect the fugitives on their perilous trip to Canada. In the interval Captain Brown was pastor, guide and counsellor. The instruction of youth he considered one of the most sacred departments of his office, so it happened that in the camp the ex-slave received his first lessons in the true principles of home-building and the responsibility of freedom. There he first heard God's commands in the words of Holy Writ:

"He hath made of one blood all the nations of the earth."

"There is no respect of persons with God."

"Do to another as you would that another should do to you."

"Remember those in bonds as bound with them."

In the field the negro learned for the first time in his life the sweetness of requited toil together with the manliness of self-defence, for the musket was companion of the implements of rural toil, as in the days of Nehemiah the restorers of Jerusalem wrought "every man with one hand upon the wall and with the other held his spear, having his sword girded by his side;" and also that it was better to die than to live a coward and a slave.

Winona was quartered at the Brown domicile. With her story and her beauty she was an object of uncommon interest to all in the camp. She became Captain Brown's special care and the rugged Puritan unbent to spoil and pet the "pretty squaw," as he delighted to call her.

And to Winona all the land had changed. The red-golden light that rested upon it near the evening hour was now as the light of heaven. The soft breezes that murmured through the trees and touched her cheek so gently, seemed to whisper, "Peace and rest. Peace and rest once again. Be not cast down."

There was the touch of sympathy and comfort in the rugged Captain's hand pressed upon her short-cropped curls. It gave her courage and robbed her heart of its cold desolation. She felt she was no longer alone; heaven, in her dire need, had sent her this good man, upon whom she might rely, in whom she could trust. Though much older, Captain Brown reminded her of her father, and her quiet childhood dependent upon him for constant companionship had given her a liking for elderly people, and she treated Captain Brown with a reverential respect that at once won his confidence and affection.

But there was not a day nor an hour that she did not think of Maxwell. She craved for news of his safety. When the daily routine of work was ended, the girl would steal into the woods which skirted the camp and climb to a seat on the high rocks watching eastward and westward for some sign of the young Englishman's return.

Winona

Some impulse of the wild things among whom she had lived drove her to a hole in under the bluff. It was necessary to descend to find it. Presently she was in a tunnel which led into a cavern. She made herself a divan of dried moss and flung herself down at full length to think. Time's divisions were lost on those days when the girl felt that she neglected no duty by hiding herself in her nook. She had come upon the eternal now as she lay in a sweet stupor until forced to arouse herself. She stared across the space that divided Maxwell from her with all the strength of her inner consciousness. That light which falls on the spot where one's loved one stands, leaving the rest of the landscape in twilight, now rested about him. With rapture she saw again the hopeless passion in Warren's eyes when he left her. Her hands and feet were cold, her muscles knotted, her face white with the force of the cry that she projected through space, "Come back to me!"

And this young creature just escaped from cruel bondage gave not a thought to the difficulties of her position. In the primal life she had led there had entered not a thought of racial or social barriers. The woods calmed her, their grays and greens and interlacing density of stems, and their whisper of a secret that has lasted from the foundation of the world, replacing her fever with the calmness of hope. In the midst of her sweet perplexity came another trouble.

Judah's capabilities were discovered very soon by Captain Brown and his sons, and he was appointed special aid and scout to the camp. Nothing could have suited him better. All day he scoured the woods, following the trail of parties of desperadoes or bringing in the fruits of the line or rifle to supply the needs in fish or meat. Twice he saved them from surprise by bands of marauders, and soon his name was heralded with that of Brown as a brave and fearless man bold to recklessness.

Sometimes Winona accompanied him on his trips when not fraught with much danger; once he tried to broach the subject nearest his heart, but a movement on her part–the carriage of the head, a queenly gesture–served to intimidate him and forced back the words.

The next night he passed in the woods, with his rifle, on a bed of leaves, studying over the problem of his life. "Why should I hesitate? We are of the same condition in life in the eyes of the world." But even while the thought was in his mind he knew that what he desired could never be. Unconsciously he was groping for the solution of the great question of social equality.

But is there such a thing as social equality? There is such a thing as the affinity of souls, congenial spirits, and good fellowship; but social equality does not exist because it is an artificial barrier which nature is constantly putting at naught by the most incongruous happenings. Who is my social equal? He whose society affords the greatest pleasure, whose tastes are congenial, and who is my brother in the spirit of the scriptural text, be he white or black, bond or free, rich or poor.

The next morning Judah built a fire in a deep ravine to cook his breakfast, and then scattered the embers that the smoke should give no sign.

All the morning he waited near her favorite haunts determined to speak out the thoughts that filled his mind. He began to fear at last that she was not coming. A little noise down the path reached his ear. In a moment he could hear slow foot-falls, and the figure of the girl parted the bushes, which closed behind her as she passed through them. She passed quite near him, walking slowly; she was very pale; her face bore traces of mental suffering. For a moment she stood there, listless, and Judah watched her with hungry eyes at a loss what to do. The sun lighted her hair, and in the upturned eyes he saw the shimmer of tears. "Winona!" He couldn't help it. The low cry broke from his lips like a groan; the next instant the girl faced him. She looked with quick wonder at the dark face with its mute appeal. Then a sudden spasm caught her throat, and left her body rigid, her hands shut, and her eyes dry and hard—she knew, instinctively, what he suffered.

"Oh, Judah! Hav'n't we been through enough without this?"

Winona

The girl trembling at the knees sank to a seat on the rocks, and folding her arms across her knees, laid her forehead against them.

"I'm going away, Winona, as soon as you are safe in Canada," he went on after a little pause. "It'll be pretty hard to leave you, but I want you to know how I've been thinking about you and sorrowing over your sorrow and hoping that you might get over your liking for Maxwell, seeing that you're only a slip of a girl, and think of me as the one who would die for you and ought naturally to care for your wants–" He spoke hesitatingly; there was a question in his last words, but the girl shook her head sadly, her tears falling to the ground. Her sorrow gave way in a great sob now, and he turned in sharp remorse and stood quite near her.

"Don't cry, Winona," he said. "I'm sorry for you and myself and Maxwell. It's this cursed slavery that's to blame. If your father had lived all this would never have happened."

"I am sorry–so very sorry! But you see, Judah, it cannot be; I have no love to give."

Judah stood beside her, his heart bursting with suppressed emotion. The bitter words would break from his lips.

"The white man gets it all–all!"

"Do you forget all that Mr. Maxwell has done for us, Judah, that you condemn him so bitterly? It is not like you–you who are generally so generous and true-hearted. He knows not of my love and will never know. Is he to blame?"

"You are right–you are right! But how is a man to distinguish between right and wrong? What moral responsibility rests upon him from whom all good things are taken? Answer me that."

They were walking now toward the camp; the shadowy trees tossed their arms in the twilight and the stars came out one by one in the sky. Only the silent tears of the girl at his side gave answer to his question.

A month had passed since the fugitives had reached the camp. Captain Brown eagerly awaited the return of Warren with Parson Steward to help them on the trip to Canada.

The wild flowers swayed above their counterfeits in every gurgling stream; the scent of wild grapes was in the air; the cliffs and rocks blossomed with purple and white and pink blooms. The birds sang and the bees droned in the woods on the morning when, wild and dishevelled, Parson Steward's wife and two children found their way into the Brown camp.

"My heavenly marster!" shrieked the widow in incoherent wailing. "The Rangers done caught my husband and shot him; they've carried the young Englishman to jail. What will become of me and my poor children?"

No one slept that night when the fate of the two gallant men was known, and the oaths uttered were not loud but deep.

Captain Brown, like a prophet of old, drew his spare form erect. Lightning flashed from his mild eyes and sword-thrusts fell from his tongue.

Then and there a rescue party was planned to take Warren out of the hands of the Philistines. The only trouble was to spy out the jail where he was confined; but there seemed little hope of success, for it appeared that since his trial Warren had disappeared from public view, and the Pro-Slavery men were very reticent. Ebenezer Maybee volunteered to secure the desired information.

As was the fashion in those days, the women listened but did not intrude their opinions upon the men, being engaged in performing the part of Good Samaritan to the widow and orphans. But long after the meeting had broken up Winona crept into the woods not to weep, but to think. She leaned against a tree and her hopeless eyes gazed down the darkening aisles; she prayed: "Help me to help save him!"

In the morning she sought an interview with Captain Brown.

CHAPTER XII

Meanwhile the wagon containing Maxwell and surrounded by constables stopped at the door of a frame building in the heart of the city, and with blows and threats Warren was pushed and dragged into a bare room and told that it was his quarters until business hours. The passageway and room were filled with a motley crowd and the vilest epithets were hurled after him. Presently a man came in with a lighted candle, seized his sound arm and looked him over from head to foot in the most insulting manner. Warren shook him off and asked him if he called himself a man to so insult a wounded stranger.

"Don't you dare speak to a white man except to answer questions, you d—d nigger-thief!"

"I shall appeal to the British consul for protection from your vile insults," said Warren in desperation. "It will cost your government dear for tonight's business."

"If you get the chance to complain," laughed the ruffian. "By G–d! you've got to die today, and by this revolver," he continued, drawing his weapon and brandishing it fiercely. He was applauded by the crowd, and it looked as if Warren were doomed when constables arriving saved further trouble. Maxwell felt that he would almost rather have been burned, than to endure the insults of such brutes.

After much entreaty, he succeeded in getting some water, but nothing more, though almost famished. Burning with fever from his wound and his contact with the funeral pile, and fainting for want of nourishment, not having tasted food since the morning before, the young man felt unable to sustain many more shocks to his system.

At length, without medical attendance, the crowd left him to get such sleep as he might upon the bare floor, without bed or covering of any kind. Retreating to a corner of the room, seated upon the floor with his back to the wall, Warren passed the hours silent and motionless.

He meditated upon his position in the heart of a hostile country although supposed to advocate and champion the most advanced ideas of liberty and human rights. What a travesty the American government was on the noblest principles! Bah! it made him heartsick. He had listened to the tales of Maybee and Steward as exaggerations; he had not believed such scenes as he had just passed through, possible in a civilized land. The words of the man who had just taunted him: "If you get the chance to complain," haunted him.

If he were not allowed to communicate with his consul, then, indeed, hope was dead. What would be his fate? The misery in store for him appalled him. And Winona–! He dared not allow his thoughts to dwell upon her. That way madness lay. So the long hours dragged out their weary length.

At eight o'clock breakfast was brought to him, and when he had begun to despair of receiving medical aid, a doctor came in and dressed his wounded arm. After this, he was marched through the streets to a room in the hotel where he was placed before the glass doors–much as is a wild beast caged in a menagerie. His reception was demoniacal. Everybody was out. Again, while en route to the seat of Justice, he endured the ignominy of oaths, yells and missiles; again the air resounded with cries of "Give him hemp!" "The rope is ready!" And so they arrived at the Court House.

The large unfinished room was filled to overflowing with the unwashed Democracy of Missouri–a roof with bare brick walls and open rafters overhead, from which hung down directly above the prisoner three new ropes with the hangman's knot at the end of each. Fierce faces, rough and dirty, with the inevitable pipe, or tobacco saliva marking the corners of the mouth, filled in the picture, while a running accompaniment of the strongest and vilest oaths ears ever heard suggested all the horrors of mob violence. The court proceeded with its farcical mockery of justice. Warren undertook to act as his own counsel, and drew up the following protest:

"I, the undersigned, a British subject, do hereby protest against every step taken thus far by the State of Missouri in this case; declaring that my rights as a British subject have been infamously violated and trampled upon.

"Warren Maxwell."

This he handed to the magistrate, who, without giving it any attention, threw it one side.

Colonel Titus and Bill Thomson were the principal witnesses against him. The Colonel told how basely the young man had betrayed his hospitality by aiding his slaves, Winona and Judah, to escape.

Thomson testified to the fact that the prisoner consorted with abolitionists of the John Brown stripe, being, when captured, in company with "fighting Steward," a red-handed criminal.

The case was given to the jury who returned a verdict of "guilty," without leaving their seats. Then followed the judge's charge and sentence:

"Warren Maxwell–It is my duty to announce to you the decision of this court as a penalty for the crime you have committed. You have been guilty of aiding slaves to run away and depart from their master's service; and now, for it you are to die!

"'Remember now thy Creator in the days of my youth,' is the language of inspired wisdom. This comes home appropriately to you in this trying moment. You are young; quite too young to be where you are. If you had remembered your Creator in your past days, you would not now be in a felon's place, to receive a felon's judgment. Still, it is not too late to remember your Creator.

"The sentence of the law is that you be taken to the State prison for one year; and that there you be closely and securely confined until Friday, the 26th day of May next; on which day, between the hours of ten in the forenoon and two in the afternoon, you will be taken to the place of public execution, and there be hanged by the neck till your body be dead. And may God have mercy on your soul!"

Overwhelmed by the mockery of a trial, Warren heard the words of the judge but they carried no meaning to his overwrought senses. He sat in a stupor until hurried by the constables to the carriage that was to convey him to prison.

Days of pain and unconsciousness followed, and when at last consciousness returned, he founded himself in a room sixteen feet square, with a small grated window at each end, through which he could catch a glimpse of the street.

Under the room in which he was confined was another of the same size, used as a lock-up for slaves who were usually put there for safe-keeping while waiting to be sent South. The room had a hole for the stove-pipe of the under room to pass through, but the stove had been removed to accommodate a larger number of prisoners. This left a hole in the floor through which one might communicate with those below. This hole in the floor afforded diversion for the invalid who could observe the full operation of the slave system. Sometimes, too, he could communicate with the slaves or some white prisoner by means of the stove-hole. When all was quiet a note was sent down through the hole, the signal being to punch with the broom-handle.

Many heart-rending scenes were enacted before his sight in the lower room. Infamous outrages were committed upon free men of color whose employment as cooks and stewards on steamers and sailing vessels had brought them within the jurisdiction of the State. Such men were usually taken ashore and sold to the highest bidder. One man who had his free papers on his person, produced them to prove the truth of his story; the official took the papers from him, burned them, and sold him the next week at public auction. Two Negroes were whipped to death rather than acknowledge the men who claimed them as their owners. One horror followed another in the crowded cage where a frightful number of human beings were herded together. They could not sleep; that is to say, forget their misery for one moment. And how hot it was already! The rays of the fierce summer sun of the South seemed to burn and sear Warren's suffering brain and dry up the healthful juices into consuming fever and ultimate madness.

One day he was aroused to greater indignation than usual by hearing heart-rending cries come from the lower room. Hurrying to the stove-hole he gazed one moment and then fell fainting with terror and nausea upon the floor. He had seen a Negro undergoing the shameful outrage, so denounced in the Scriptures, and which must not be described in the interests of decency and humanity.

That night Maxwell was again ill–delirious–requiring the care of two physicians and a slave who was detailed to nurse him.

Unhappily we tell no tale of fiction. We have long felt that the mere arm of restraint is but a temporary expedient for the remedy, but not the prevention, of cruelty and crime. If Christianity, Mohammedanism, or even Buddhism, did exercise the gentle and humanizing influence that is claimed for them, these horrors would cease now that actual slavery has been banished from our land; because, as religion is the most universal and potent source of influence upon a nation's action, so it must mould to some extent its general characteristics and individual opinions. Until we can find a religion that will give the people individually and practically an impetus to humane and unselfish dealing with each other, look to see outward forms change, but never look to see the spirit which hates and persecutes that which it no longer dare enslave, changed by any other influence than a change of heart and spirit.

The liberties of a people are not to be violated but with the wrath of God. Indeed, we tremble for our country when we reflect that God is just; that His justice cannot sleep forever; that considering natural means only, a revolution of the wheel of Fortune, an exchange of situation is among the possibilities.

All through the long delirium of pain and weariness Warren was conscious of the tender care of his nurse. To the sick man the wearing, jarring sound of voices rising out of a black pit was ever present and unbearable. At times they were to him the cries of the ruffians who pursued him to the stake; the vengeance of the mob seemed to fill the little room and charge the atmosphere with horror. Again it was the sound of the pistol shot that killed Parson Steward, and the patient would shudder at the blood everywhere—on shirts, hands and faces, and splashing the sides of the bare walls; or it was the flames mounting higher and higher, licking his body with hungry tongues, or it was the rushing of whirling waters against the vessel's side as he swung Winona over the side of "Crescent."

Finally, as he lay tossing and tormented with these phantom terrors in his eyes and ears, the sound died away into the soft hush of a tender voice stilling the tumult.

The nurse was a young mulatto known as Allen Pinks. The boy had been cook and head-waiter on board a steamboat on the Missouri river. He had been paid off, according to his story, at St. Joseph. From there he had started for Leavenworth, walking down the Missouri bank of the river with a white man. At the ferry he was stopped on suspicion of being a fugitive slave and lodged in the calaboose; from there he was removed to the State prison until the time of sale. He had made himself very useful about the jail doing chores and nursing the sick, for which he seemed to have a particular vocation. Very soon Allen Pinks was a great favorite and allowed many privileges; hearing of Maxwell's illness he asked to be allowed to nurse him, and the jailer was more than glad to have him do it.

At last there came a day when the prisoner's wild wide eyes were closed, and the boy rose from his long watch by the side of the rude cot bed with hope in his heart. He stood, for a second, looking down upon the calm face of the sleeper with a sorrowful smile on his dark brown face. "Fast asleep at last," he whispered. "I must go see to his broth."

Just then a hideous yell arose from the room below. With a light bound the lad reached the stove-hole.

"Hush your noise!" he called in a low tone of authority. "Haven't I told you he must sleep?"

"Got a black boss dis time," came up from the hole in a gruff voice, followed by a low laugh.

"He's asleep now, and everything depends on his waking up right. But you set up a howl that would wake the dead!"

"Howl? dat's singing," came again from the hole in the floor.

"Well, keep your singing to yourself."

The noise subsided, and the young nurse turned again to his patient.

He stood for some moments gazing down on the Saxon face so pitifully thin and delicate. The brow did not frown nor the lips quiver; no movement of the muscles betrayed the hopeless despair of the sleeper's heart. The cot gave a creak and a rustle. The nurse was leaning one hand on the edge of the miserable pallet bed bending over the sick man. There was a light touch on his hair; a tear fell on his cheek; the nurse had kissed the patient!

When the door had closed behind the lad, Warren opened his eyes in full consciousness; and as he brushed the tear from his face, there came a puzzled look into his eyes.

Presently Allen returned with the soup and found him awake. His features lighted up with intelligence and sympathy on making the discovery, and finding him free from fever.

"Well, how are you getting on, sir?" he asked in the softest of musical voices, and feeling Warren's pulse, as he seated himself on a stool at the bedside.

"Who are you? Haven't I met you somewhere? Your voice has a familiar sound."

"I fancy you don't know me," replied Allen with a smile.

"You've saved my life."

"That's a subject we won't speak of just now, sir; you must be very quiet."

"Oh, to be well and free once more!" broke in a plaintive tone from the invalid.

"If you will only remain quiet and easy in your mind, there's no doubt all may yet be well," replied the boy with significant emphasis as he held Warren's eye a second with a meaning gaze.

Many questions came crowding to Warren's lips; but Allen silenced him firmly and gently.

"Bye and bye, sir, I will tell you all I can, but you must drink this broth now and sleep."

Warren drank the soup and with a feeling of peace new to him, turned his face to the wall and slept.

One week longer Warren lay on his rude bed. Allen refused to talk but told him that he had no cause for anxiety.

Maxwell was fascinated by his nurse; he thought him the prettiest specimen of boyhood he had ever met. The delicate brown features were faultless in outline; the closely cropped black hair was like velvet in its smoothness. He could not shake off the idea that somewhere he had known the lad before in his life. At times this familiarity manifested itself in the tones of the voice soft and low as a woman's, then again it was in the carriage of the head or the flash of the beautiful large dark eyes. It was an evasive but haunting memory.

One day Allen said: "Mr. Maxwell, I'm not to tend you any longer after this week. I'm to be sold."

"Sold!" ejaculated Warren in dismay.

Allen nodded. "It's getting too hot for me, and I'm going to run for it."

"What shall I do without you?" said Warren with a sick feeling of despair at his heart.

"Have you no hope of escape? Have you never thought of being rescued?" asked the lad in a whisper with a cautious motion of the hand toward the door.

"Oh, Allen!" faltered Warren in speechless joy.

The lad gave him time to recover himself a bit; then, after glancing around the corridor to see that no one was listening, returned to his patient.

"I am here in the interest of your friends! I leave tonight. Tomorrow you will receive a communication from your friends. We must hasten our plans for Thomson is expected on a visit here any day."

"Go on; go on; tell me what to do."

"There is nothing for you to do but to be ready at a moment's notice. The plans are all well laid, and will be successful, unless Thomson should upset us."

"I fear that man," replied Warren with a shudder.

"You certainly have good reason," said Allen. "But he does not reside in this vicinity and we may be able to avoid him."

"He would be only too happy to wreak his vengeance upon me. Yes, I fear him."

Allen did his best to reassure Warren, and discussed with him the plan of escape as far as he knew it, and concluded by saying:

"I shall not see you again. Keep up your heart. Barring accident, you will soon be free."

At night Allen went as usual to the well to draw the water for supper, and did not return. The alarm was given, but no trace of the boy was found.

CHAPTER XIII

The next morning dawned hot and sultry; all day there were signs of a thunder storm.

Towards dark the door of Warren's cell opened and a young man with a carpet bag, apparently in a great hurry to catch a train, and accompanied by the jailer, came to the grated door and informed Warren that he had been requested by the British consul at New York, who had heard of his case, to see him and to say to him that his case would be investigated and all done that could be done, and that he would hear from the consul in person in a few days.

The visitor was quite curious about the hall, looking around a great deal, and as he stood with his back to the grated door talking to the jailer, whose attention he directed to some means of ventilation outside, Warren saw a small slip of paper in the hand which he held behind him, and took it.

When he was alone again, he unfolded it with trembling fingers. It contained the words: "Be ready at midnight." Scarcely had he recovered from the excitement which the note caused him, when he heard footsteps and voices again approaching his cell and in a few seconds the sallow, uncanny face of Bill Thomson was framed in the doorway.

"It seems to me, you fellows ain't as careful as you might be. Had a visitor sent by the British consul, did he? Well that won't save his neck. I tell you, Bub," he said, directly addressing the prisoner, "saltpetre won't save you. You've got to go, by G–d. D–n these newspaper men I say; a set of ornery skunks; meddling with business that don't consarn 'em. But they don't euchre me this deal."

Warren made no answer, and in a short time the visitor passed on. With senses strained to their utmost tension, he watched the shades of night envelope the landscape. He listened to the striking of the clock in the corridor outside his cell, tolling the lagging hours, with beating heart. Gradually all sound died away and the hush of night fell upon the earth, broken only by the fury of the storm which now broke scattering destruction in its wake. Far off the river sounded a mimic Niagara as it swelled beyond its boundaries. In the midst of his anxiety the young man noted the strange coincidence of the storms which had attended three critical periods in his history while in America. With this thought in his mind he heard the clock toll off twelve strokes. As the last one died slowly away there came a thundering knock at the outer prison door. It came again, and yet again. He heard a door slam and then the voice of the jailer, "What do you want?"

"We are from Andrew County, with a prisoner we want put in jail for safe keeping."

"Who is he?"

"A notorious horse thief."

"Have you a warrant?"

"No; but it's all right."

"I can't take a man without authority."

"If you don't it will be too bad; he's a desperate character, and we've had hard work to catch him. We'll satisfy you in the morning that it's all right."

The jailer went down and let them in. When they were inside where the light fell upon their faces he started back with the cry:

"It's Allen Pinks!"

The men with him were Maybee and old John Brown.

"Yes, Mr. Owens," said Captain Brown grimly, "it's the boy, and it's too late to make a noise. If you resist or give an alarm, you are a dead man. The lower door is guarded, and the jail surrounded by an armed force."

Warren beheld the scene from between the bars of his cell door with anxious heart; even as he looked he saw a dark object pass behind the group and advance along the corridor wall, but his attention was drawn from the shadow as a door opened far down the row and Bill Thomson, fully dressed, faced the group, pistol in hand.

He advanced step by step with his eyes fixed upon the negro lad. The boy involuntarily uttered a cry and covered his face with his hands.

"Well, sir! if it ain't Winona! Looks interestin', Owens, that you couldn't tell a gal dressed up in boys clo's! This strikes me heavy."

Warren standing helpless in his cell saw and heard all, and understood many things that had puzzled him. There are loves and loves; but Warren told himself that the love of the poor forsaken child before him was of the quality which we name celestial. All the beauty and strength of the man, and every endowment of tenderness came upon him there as the power came upon Samson; and he registered a promise before heaven that night.

"Halt!" cried Captain Brown, as Thomson moved a step nearer. "Halt, or you're a dead man!"

"So it is murder you propose to commit?"

"No; we have come in peace, if let alone, to rescue our friend Maxwell. If you interfere with us the worst is your own. Disarm him, Mr. Maybee."

But Thomson aimed his pistol straight at Winona's breast, and cried: "I fire if you come a step nearer."

Warren groaned. "Oh, for a moment's freedom and a good weapon in my hand!"

Suddenly a lurid glare lighted up the hall, and Warren saw a dark shadow creeping in Thomson's rear. Something of an extraordinary nature was about to happen.

"It is Judah! It is Judah!"

It was indeed Judah. He had crept along gradually advancing nearer and nearer, bending almost double in observation; then like a wild beast preparing to pounce upon his prey, he stiffened his powerful muscles, and with a bound sprang upon Thomson, seizing him in an iron grasp, and dragging him backward to the ground with such violence that his pistol flew from his hand. Placing one foot upon the breast of the prostrate man to prevent him from rising, he picked up the pistol, crying:

"It is between you and me, now. Our roles are reversed. It is you who must die."

He was about to fire, when Captain Brown hastily interfered:

"No, no; it won't do. Spare him!"

"Spare him! For what? To afford him an opportunity to do more mischief? No, No!"

"Let us release Maxwell first and get outside the building then, if you insist upon this thing," said Maybee.

"Quick, then! I will not answer for myself. Your safety is not the only thing to be considered; I must think of myself as well. If I do not kill this man, he will murder me by inches if I fall into his hands, as he has already tried to do. I hate him, I hate him! It is my enemy I would slay, not yours."

(To be continued.)

CHAPTER XIII.–(Concluded.)

With a rapid movement he stooped, placed the barrel of his pistol at Thomson's forehead and–would have pulled the trigger but for the interference of John Brown, who threw himself upon the enraged black and stayed his hand.

"Don't do it; not this time, Judah. I know your feelings, but you'll have another chance, for these fellows will be after us again. There's too much at stake now; we owe Mr. Maxwell something for all he has suffered. Don't do it."

"Yes," chimed in Maybee; "if you let up now, Judah, I'll be tee-totally smashed if I don't lend you a hand and stand by for fair play."

"Why stay my hand? Vengeance is sweet," replied Judah, his dark, glowing eyes fixed in a threatening gaze upon his foe bound and helpless at his feet.

"There is a time for everything, my son. Stay thy hand and fear not; vengeance is mine," said John Brown.

Judah was silent for a moment, but stood as if gathering strength to resist temptation. Finally he said:

"I am the Lord's instrument to kill this man. Promise me that when this villain's life shall lie in the gift of any man in the camp, he shall be given to me as my right, to deal with him as I see fit."

"We promise," broke from Captain Brown and Ebenezer Maybee simultaneously.

Sternly the determined trio, aided by Winona in her boy's attire, secured the officials of the jail and quieted the prisoners. It was hard to resist the entreaties of the slaves confined there, but, after a hurried consultation, it was deemed advisable not to burden themselves with fugitive slaves.

With few words the business of releasing Maxwell was carried forward. When Maybee unlocked the door of Warren's cell with the warden's key, there were tears in his eyes as he beheld the wreck that two months of imprisonment and brutal treatment had made of the stalwart athlete. The burns were not yet healed, and great red scars disfigured his face in spots; he still wore his arm in a sling; starvation, physical weakness and lack of cleanliness had done their worst.

Maybee's heart was too full for words as he folded the emaciated form in his arms, and openly wiped the tears from his eyes; his were the feelings of a father: "This, my son, was dead and is alive again."

"Oh, never m-min' my cryin'! 'Taint nothin'. Some fellers cries easier than others," he muttered as the tears rolled unchecked down his cheeks. Winona was sobbing in company and Judah was feeling strange about the eyes also.

"I never thought to see you again, boys" said Warren solemnly, as he held their warm, friendly hands and felt the clasp of honest friendship. "I understand the slavery question through and through. Experience is a stern teacher."

"Min' my words to you, Maxwell? But God knows I didn't reckon they'd come home to you so awful an' suddint-like. I have never feared for you, my boy, even when things l-looked blackes'; but if you don' fin' Bill Thomson somewhere, some time, an' choke him an' tear his win'pipe to fiddlestrings, you ain't got a drop of British blood in yer whole carcass!"

"Amen!" ejaculated Captain Brown. "Come, boys, time's up."

Judah lifted Maxwell in his strong arms preparatory to carrying him out to the waiting vehicle. He felt all his passionate jealousy die a sudden death as pity and compassion stirred his heart for the sufferings of his rival. "Here is another white man who does not deserve death at a Negro's hands," he told himself.

Winona was silent and constrained in manner. For the first time since she had adopted her strange dress she felt a wave of self-consciousness that rendered her ashamed. She turned mechanically and walked by Judah's side as he bore his almost helpless burden to the wagon, and seated herself beside the driver, still silent.

Warren, reclining on fresh straw in the bottom of the cart, wondered in semi-consciousness at the sweetness of the air dashed in his face with the great gusts of rain, and at his own stupidity in not recognizing Winona; beneath the stain with which she had darkened her own exquisite complexion, he could now plainly trace the linaments that had so charmed him. Then, lulled by the motion of the vehicle and weakened by excitement, he slept the sleep of exhaustion.

Captain Brown had ordered the prisoners placed in Warren's abandoned cell, and, locking the door, took the key with them to clog the movements of pursuers as much as possible; then they passed out, closing and fastening the great outer door and also taking that key with them.

Meanwhile, outside the building, in the most advantageous positions, hidden by the blackness of the night, ten stalwart Free-State men had waited with impatience the return of Captain Brown and his companions.

The storm favored the rescuing party; not a sound disturbed their watch but the awful peals of thunder reverberating over the land in solemn majesty. Torrents of rain drenched them to the skin, but inured to hardships they rejoiced in the favor which the storm bestowed.

As the rescuers issued from beneath the jail's shadow, Judah bearing Warren in his arms, the guard gathered silently about the wagon in silent congratulation that thus far they had been successful; then mounting their waiting horses, the whole party rode as fast as possible toward the river.

As dawn approached the storm cleared, and the first faint streaks of light that appeared in the east were tinged with the sun-god's brilliant hues. By this time our party had reached the riverbanks, and Warren was removed to the boat, the horses and wagon being returned to the friendly settlers who had loaned them, and in the sweet freshness of the dawn, strong arms propelled the boat toward the Kansas shore.

On the Kansas side fresh horses awaited them and another wagon. Friends met them at short intervals along the route, the people turning out en masse in an ovation to the rescuers and rescued, for Maxwell's story was known in every village and town throughout the country. They stopped at a comfortable farmhouse for breakfast, and Warren was allowed the luxury of a bath and given clean though coarse clothing.

They travelled all day and night, seeming not to feel fatigue but bent upon distancing a pursuing party, finding fresh horses at intervals, and food in abundance. Thus the settlers exemplified in kind acts the sympathy that upheld the common cause of human rights for all mankind.

The journey to the Brown camp was not a short one, and burdened with an invalid, it added to the length of time necessary to make the trip. Every step, too, was fraught with danger, but not a murmur came from the men who with stern faces and senses alert cautiously picked their way to safety. It was still twenty miles across country as the crow flies, after three days of swift travelling; the meandering of the road added five more. Then there was a barrier of foothills, and finally the mountains which lifted themselves abruptly out of the flat rolling surface surrounding them.

There might be marauding parties hiding in the brush and thickets, and for aught the horsemen knew, the stacks of hay and fodder that rose like huge monuments on every side, out of the twilight gloom surrounding the lonely farms, might conceal dozens of their foes. The nights were wearing for they never knew quite how the situation was going to develop.

Most of the time Warren was in a semi-conscious state exciting fears of a return of fever and delirium. The sight of guns and the constant talk of the battle yet to come had a depressing effect upon the invalid; they gave a sinister effect to his freedom. Soon the smiling sunlit valley they were entering became to his disordered fancy a return into the dangers and sufferings of a Missouri prison.

Much to Captain Brown's relief, the late afternoon found them in the pleasant hollow two miles distant from the camp, and night gave them safety within the shadow of the great hills.

Winona

CHAPTER XIV

The physical shock to Maxwell's system had worked no lasting harm to his constitution. Freedom, cleanliness and nourishing food were magical in their effects, and a week after his rescue found him up and about gradually joining in the duties of the camp.

And what an experience it was to this young, tenderly nurtured aristocrat! It was his function to watch the shifting panorama of defiance to despotism as outlined in the daily lives of the patriotic abolitionists with whom his lot was now cast. He lived in an atmosphere of suspicion, for to be identified with John Brown was a forfeit of one's life; a price was on the head of every individual associated with him. Yet with all the discouraging aspects of the cause these men had espoused, scarcely a day went by that did not bring news of the movement of the enemy, sent by some friendly well-wisher, or a token of good feeling in the form of much needed supplies, and even delicacies for the sick.

The menace of impending danger, however, hung over them constantly. The very ground was honey-combed with intrigue set on foot by resolute and determined Southerners who vowed to crush out all opposition and make the institution of slavery national, and with this determination conspiracies of every kind were abroad to circumvent the North and its agents, of whom the Kansas pro-slavery men were the most belligerent, in the growing desire of that section to make freedom universal within the borders of the United States. He saw plainly that the nation was fast approaching an alarming crisis in its affairs, and, by contrast with the arguments and attitude of the South, that the weight of principle was with the North where the people had been alarmingly docile and conservative. The efforts, in Congress, and in pro-slavery political conventions, were but an aggravation, and not satisfactory to either side, adding fuel to the flame that was making terrible inroads upon the public peace.

The Brown men were restless because of enforced inactivity, for all felt a blow was impending, marvelling that it was so long delayed,

113

and anxious to force an issue–anything was better than uncertainty– for the lengthened time of waiting was a terrible strain upon the nerves.

Captain Brown sought the company of Maxwell frequently, conversing freely of his hopes and fears. The young man was greatly impressed with the clearness and value of his knowledge of military tactics. He was familiar with all the great battles of ancient and modern times; had visited every noted battlefield of old Europe and carefully sketched plans of the operations and positions of the opposing forces. These maps were a source of delight to the old man who went over them with Warren, explaining with great enthusiasm the intricacies of the manœuvres. During this intimacy, Captain Brown revealed to his guest his own great scheme for an insurrection among the slaves–an uprising of such magnitude that it should once and for all time settle the question of slavery.

Maxwell promised money and ammunition and arms, but his heart was heavy as he listened to plans and purposes that had been long in maturing, brooded over silently and secretly, with much earnest thought, and under a solemn sense of religious duty. What would be the fate of the band of hero-martyrs who would dash themselves to bloody death under the inspired influence of their intrepid leader? The prison walls would shake from summit to foundation, and wild alarm would fill every tyrant heart in all the South, of this he had no doubt, but would the effort be crowned with success? It was hardly possible.

Summer was advancing ever deeper in dust. The sky was tarnishing with haze. The sunsets longer in burning out in the west, in tragic colors. Scouts were continually posting back and forth. Warren had promised himself while in prison never to complain of the dispensations of Providence should he live to enjoy freedom again; but at the end of the second week of convalescence he was imploring to be allowed to join the scouting parties of skirmishers. The stir of the camp fired his blood; he was devoured by anxiety to be among the busy people of the world once more, to know what events had transpired in his absence and how the world had wagged along without his help, forgetting that a vacuum is quickly filled and we are soon forgotten.

"The sooner I get out of this the better, Maybee;" he exclaimed one day, rousing himself from painful memories of home and his failure to accomplish the mission he had set out so confidently to perform. "I want to get home!"

"Jest so," replied Maybee, with ready sarcasm. "We'll start tomorrow morning on foot."

"No—you know what I mean. I want to—"

"Oh, yes, cert'nly; jest so. We might, ef you're in a great hurry, start this evenin'. The Rangers are all over the place between here an' civilization, but we won't stop for that, for with a strong fightin' man like you fer a companion there'd be nothin' to fear—about gittin' a through ticket to glory this week."

"Cease jesting, Maybee! What I want is to make every hour tell upon the work of getting well—not only on my own account, but—we owe that poor girl something."

"Hem!" grunted Maybee, shooting the young man a keen look under which he colored slightly. "That's right; always keep the weaker vessel in yer mem'ry; trust in the Lord and keep yer powder dry, as our friend Brown'd say. And that remin's me of 'Tarius up home. 'Tarius got religion and when the day came roun' fer the baptism' it was a January blizzard, although well along in the month of April. 'Tarius ain't fond of cold weather no how, and he didn't show up along with the other candidates. Next day the minister came up to look after 'Tarius. 'Don' ye trus' in de Lawd, brother?' says the minister. 'Yes, brother,' says Tarius, 'I trust pintedly in de Lawd; but I ain't gwine fool wif God!' That's my advice to you, Maxwell; don't you fool with Providence; jest let well-enough alone."

The next afternoon Mr. Maybee came rushing back to the cabin which was their mutual home.

"Well, young feller, we're in fer it, an' no mistake. You'll git fightin' a-plenty before forty-eight hours."

"What's it?" queried Maxwell languidly, "another false alarm?"

"No, by gosh; it's the real thing this time. The Rangers are at Carlton's. You remember hearin' Parson Steward speak of Reynolds don' you?" Maxwell nodded.

"He's come up to camp an' brought Brown the news."

"How soon will they get here?"

"Cayn't tell; maybe tomorrow an' perhaps not before nex' week; but it's boun' to come. Dog my cats, if I'm sorry. I fairly itch to git my hands on the onery cusses that killed the parson."

"Anything is better than waiting; it takes the life out of a man. I shall not feel safe until I get my feet on British soil once more. God being my helper, Maybee, I'll never set foot on the soil of the 'greatest (?) Republic on earth' again," he finished earnestly.

Mr. Maybee chuckled.

"Con-vinced are you? They used ter tell me when I was a little shaver that the proof of the puddin' was in swallerin' the bag—that is, pervidin' it was a biled puddin'. I'll 'low them varmints heat you pretty hot, but there's nothin so convincin' as ex-perience. I might a talked to you fer forty days an' nights, wastin' my breath fer nothin', an' you'd a said to yourself 'Maybee's stretchin' it; 'taint quarter so bad as he makes out;' but jest as soon as they git to work on your anatermy yer fin' out that Maybee was mild by comparison. The South's a horned hornet on the 'nigger' question. Time n'r tide, n'r God A'mighty aint goin' to change 'em this week."

"Well, I'm ready for them; I'm feeling decidedly fit," replied Maxwell.

"Good. Reynolds left you a message, a sort of warning. Thomson says the nex' time he gits you he'll fix you, law or no law; he's goin' to flog you first like a nigger, an' then burn you an' send your ashes to your folks in England in a chiny vase. How's that strike you?"

"He will if he's lucky; but I have my doubts."

Maybee gazed at him in silent admiration a moment before he said: "British grit a plenty in you, by thunder; that's the talk."

Preparations immediately went forward in the camp for meeting the enemy. Winona's cave on the mountainside was to be stored with provision, ammunition and all other necessaries. The men worked all night in detachments, watch and watch.

Warren had seen very little of Winona; she kept with the women.

Thinking of the coming conflict, Warren climbed the slope leading to the top of the highest peak, and established himself there as a lookout. It was near the cave in which supplies were being stored, and where the women and children would find a refuge. Presently he saw Winona loitering up the hillside with downcast eyes. As she drew near, the magnetism of his gaze compelled her glance to seek his face. She started, and would have turned back but Warren called out in a kindly voice not in the least alarming:

"Come, see this fine sweep of country. We cannot be surprised."

The sudden blush that had suffused her cheek at sight of him died out, leaving her serious and calm. The last few days she had thawed somewhat out of her coldness, for care could not live with youth and gaiety and the high-tide of summer weather, and the propinquity, morning, noon and night, of the society of the well-beloved one.

More and more Warren felt toward her as to a darling, irresistible child, and sometimes as to a young goddess far beyond him, as he realized how pure and sweet the inner life of this childwoman. The noisome things that creep and crawl about the life of the bond chattel

117

had fallen away from her. She was unique: a surprise every day in that she was innocence personified and yet so deliciously womanly,

> "Standing, with reluctant feet,
> Where the brook and river meet,
> Womanhood and childhood fleet!"

In this last week of returning strength, Winona imagined, when she saw Maxwell sitting among the men of the camp moody and silent, that he was remembering his home with longing and awaiting the moment for safe departure with impatience.

During her weeks of unselfish devotion when she had played the role of the boy nurse so successfully, she had been purely and proudly glad. Now, little by little, a gulf had opened between them which to her unsophisticated mind could not be bridged. There lay the misery of the present time–she was nothing to him. Does any love resign its self-imposed tasks of delightful cares and happy anxieties without a pang? Like any other young untrained creature, she tormented herself with fears that were but shadows and railed at barriers which she herself had raised, even while she argued that Fate had fixed impassable chasms of race and caste between them.

"How a man glories in war," she said, after a silence, from her seat on a jagged rock overhanging the cliff.

"You, with your Indian training, ought to feel with us and not think of fear," said Warren.

"But then, I am not of the blood."

"True."

His reply fell upon her ear like a reproach–a reflection upon her Negro origin. Her suspicion sounded in her voice as she replied:

"Better an Indian than a Negro? I do not blame you for your preference."

"Why speak with that tone—so scornfully? Is it possible that you can think so meanly of me?"

She could not meet his eye, but her answer was humbly given—her answer couched in the language of the tribes.

"Are you not a white brave? Do not all of them hate the black blood?"

"No; not all white men, thank God. In my country we think not of the color of the skin but of the man—the woman—the heart."

"Oh, your country! Do you know, I believe my dear papa was of the same?"

Her head rested against the tree back of her; the lace-work of the pine ashes formed upon her knees and enveloped her as a cloud.

He nodded in reply, and continued, musingly, as his eyes wandered off over the plain at his feet:

"England is a country to die for—rich, grand, humane! You shall see it for yourself."

"Which is my country, I wonder? Judah says that he will not fight for the Stars and Stripes if war comes—the flag that makes the Negro a slave. This country mine? No, no! The fearful things that I have seen—" she broke off abruptly. "My father's country shall be mine."

"Better reserve your decision until you marry."

"I shall never marry."

"But why?" asked Warren, opening his eyes in surprise. "Nonsense; all girls expect to marry, and do—most of them."

"I cannot marry out of the class of my father," she replied, with head proudly erect. "It follows, then, that I shall never marry."

"Nonsense," again returned Warren. "You will not live and grow old alone. Mere birth does not count for more than one's whole training afterward, and you have been bred among another race altogether."

"But the degradation of the two years just passed can never leave me; life will never seem quite the same," she said in a stifled voice full of pain. "I shall be a nun." She ended with a little laugh, but the voice quivered beneath it.

Warren scarcely knew how to answer her; he felt awkward and mere words sounded hollow.

"See here," he began abruptly; "it is no use to dwell on a painful subject; just strive to forget all about it and take the happiness that comes your way. As for the last alternative—you will not be happy."

"That cannot be helped. Perhaps I should not be happy if I married," she went on with a smile upon her lips, but deep gravity in her eyes. "It would depend upon the man who must know all my past. Nokomis used to say 'they are all the same—the men. When you are beautiful they kill each other for you; when you are plain they sneer at you.'"

"Old Nokomis! She spoke of red men, not white men."

"Yes; all the same Nokomis said: men are men. People will never forget that my mother was an American Negress even if I forget. No," concluded the girl with a wise little shake of her cropped head, "I shall go to the convent."

Warren dissembled his intense amusement, but beneath his smile was a tear for the tender, helpless creature trying so bravely to crush out of sight the tender flowers of her maiden heart. At length he said:

"Who can foresee the future? There are men with red blood in their veins; not all are empty caskets. How can you talk of convents—you who will go to England with me; and perhaps, who can tell, you may marry a duke. But believe me, Winona, you think too seriously of your position," he concluded, dropping his jesting air.

>   "'You have too much respect upon the world:
>   They lose it that do buy it with much care.'"

Silence fell between them for a time, and the evening shadows gradually shut the eye of day. Clear and shrill upon the air fell the notes of a bugle, once–twice–thrice–it rose in warning cadence. Winona sprang to her feet with the words, "'Tis Judah! There is danger! Let us go at once!"

So violent was her start that she came perilously near falling to the plain below, which on this side the hill was a sheer descent of many feet, to where the Possawatomie rilled along its peaceful course.

"God!" broke from Warren's white lips as he caught her just in time. For a second he held her in a close embrace, she clinging to him in affright. There was extraordinary gravity in both look and tone as he leaned his cheek against the cropped curly head that nestled close to his throat like a frightened child, and said: "Winona, let me say it now before we go to meet we know not what–thank God I have known you–so noble, so patient, so sweet. Despite the dangers of our situation, the hours we have passed together have been the happiest of my life."

Forgetful of time and place, youth yielded to the sway of the love-god, and for one dazzling instant the glory of heaven shone upon them.

"What harm just once?" thought the girl as she rested in his embrace. "Tomorrow it may not matter about race or creed, one or both of us will belong to eternity; pray God that I may be the one to go."

CHAPTER XV

It was not Judah who had blown the warning blast, but it came from one of his party sent by him to warn them of the approach of the enemy. The messenger was pale as death, the veins standing out on his forehead, and his left arm hanging useless at his side. The horse, panting and covered with foam, stopped, and Maybee caught the rider in his arms.

"What is it, boy?" he asked.

"Rangers," the poor fellow gasped out. "Three hundred around the old farmhouse. Coming down on you. Judah says he can hold them off until daybreak. I got out, but they shot me."

Captain Brown seemed transformed; his eyes burned like coals. Maybee put his hand on his shoulder.

"What'll you do, Captain, start now or later?"

"Two hours after midnight. The boy knows his business," was the laconic reply as, drawing long, deep breaths, John Brown made for the horses.

The evening was spent in preparations for the start. The camp was abandoned, the women hastily fleeing to the refuge on the mountainside. Three men were to be left to guard the cave, but every woman carried a rifle in her hand and was prepared to use it. Winona was in command of the home-guard.

The last words of counsel and instruction were spoken. It was nearly daylight. Faint streaks of light were already visible in the eastern horizon. They left the camp two hours after midnight and the last look that Warren gave toward the mountain showed him the slight figure of Winona with rifle in hand waving him a farewell salute.

To Maxwell the one hundred intrepid riders, with whom he was associated, represented a hopeless cause. How could they hope to conquer a force of three hundred desperadoes? But Warren knew not the valor of his companions nor the terror which the Brown men inspired.

The attacking point was an hour's fast riding from camp. The dawn increased rapidly. Maybee fell back to Warren's side with an air of repressed excitement, and his eyes blazed. He touched the young man's arm as they rode and pointed to the left where they saw, in a cloud of dust, another party of horsemen coming toward them.

"Who are they, friends or enemies?"

"Reinforcements. They are the boys Reynolds has collected to help us. Nothing the matter with him or them, you bet. Reynolds ain't been the same since Steward was killed. His heart's broke 'long with it an' he's wil' fer revenge. Every one of the boys with him is a fighter, too, from 'way back. I know 'em, Maxwell; an' now, — me, if we don't give them hell-hounds the biggest thrashing they've had since the campaign opened, you may call me a squaw. But who's that riding beside Reynolds?" he broke off abruptly. "Dog my cats, may I be teetotally smashed ef it don't look like Parson Steward!"

"No!" cried Warren in a fever of excitement at the words. "Impossible!"

"We'll soon know," replied Maybee.

On they sped over the space that separated the two parties. Then the order came to halt, and Parson Steward rode into the midst of the column while the men broke into wild cheering at sight of him. There was not much time to spend in greeting, but the vice-like grip of friendly hands spoke louder than words. Warren could not speak for a moment as before his mind the picture of the last night spent in Steward's company passed vividly. The parson, too, was visibly affected.

"Praise God from whom all blessings flow," he said solemnly.

"Amen," supplemented Maxwell, then they rode cautiously forward, the Captain keeping his men at the steady pace at which they had started out. Now and then a stray shot from the farmhouse showed them that Judah was holding his own. The firing increased as they neared the house, coming mainly from the shelter of trees and bushes at the side. Finally it became incessant, and the Captain beckoned to Maybee, after he had halted the column, and they rode cautiously ahead. Soon they returned, and coming to Warren drew him to the flank of the company.

"My boy, you are going under fire. Are you prepared for any happening? Are you all right?"

"All right," replied Warren.

"Well," said Captain Brown with a sigh, "shake hands; fire low; look well to the hinder side of your rifle. God bless you!" and he passed forward to the head of the column. The parson went with him.

Maybee was beside himself with excitement over the parson's rescue.

"Now you'll see some fun," said he; and then, all of a sudden the fire of battle caught him and he flew into a sort of frenzy. He rode quickly behind the men, saying in low, concentrated tones: "Give 'em — boys! Remember our friends they've butchered, and our women and little children. Give 'em —, I say!" Then growing calmer he turned to Warren once more, saying: "Maxwell, I reckon you've got as big a score to settle as anyone of us." Then he, too, wrung Warren's hand and rode away to the head of the column.

A man fell dead in the Brown ranks. The Rangers now advanced in solid column to meet them. Then came the order to charge, and with a wild yell the pent-up excitement of the men broke forth and pell-mell they hurled themselves upon the foe.

Then ensued a wild scene; a turmoil of shots, cries, groans and shrieks–pandemonium on earth. Maxwell very soon found himself in the thickest of it, off his horse and doing his part in a fierce hand-to-hand encounter with one who had fired a pistol straight at him. The bullet flew wide of the mark and in an instant he had flung the snarling demon down and had hurled himself upon him. They struggled fiercely back and forth tearing at each other with all their might. Gideon Holmes' long, lithe fingers were sunk deep in his throat in an endeavor to force him to release his hold. With a mighty effort, Maxwell brought the butt of his pistol down on his enemy's face in a smashing blow. At last he had caught the full spirit of the fiercest; the blood mounted to his brain, and with ungovernable rage, thinking only of the sufferings he had endured in the dreadful time of imprisonment, he continued his rain of blows upon his prostrate foe until the very limpness of the inert body beneath him stayed his hand.

Through the smoke he saw Captain Brown and Parson Steward and Ebenezer Maybee fighting like mad, with blazing rifles, and deep curses from Maybee mingling with the hoarse shouting of passages of Scripture by the parson.

"Behold, the uncircumcised Philistine, how he defies the armies of the living God." And again–"Let no man's heart fail because of him; thy servant will go and fight with this Philistine;" "Fear not, neither be thou dismayed."

It was a terrible struggle between the two great forces–Right and Wrong. Drunken with vile passions, the Rangers fought madly but in vain against the almost supernatural prowess of their oponents; like the old Spartans who braided their hair and advanced with songs and dancing to meet the enemy, the anti-slavery men advanced singing hymns and praising God.

The last stand was made. The desperadoes fled in all directions. Some went toward the hills; among them was Thomson. He spurred his horse across the plain, abandoning him at the edge of the rising ground. For hours he skulked among the trees or crawled or crept over stones and through bushes, gradually rising higher and higher above the plain. Brown's forces swarmed over the ground, slaying as they met the flying foe. He saw Col. Titus pursued by Judah, speeding over the plain; he saw them meet and the Colonel fall. A moment–a moment–a convulsive uplifting of arms, and then Judah turned and slowly began climbing the ascent.

Thomson, regardless of consequences, sprang clear of the underbrush and darted up the mountainside. Once he thought he heard a rifle crack–on–on he sped. He climbed upon a ledge and lay there, peeping through a crevice made by the meeting of gigantic rocks, and gaining his breath. He saw no one. Evidently Judah had missed him, and he began to plan a descent from the opposite side. Searching the cliff for a landing place, he saw the Possawatamie gurgling along sixty feet below over pebbles, a torrent in winter but now only a silver thread that trickled lightly along.

He saw a jutting ledge ten feet below which promised an easy footing to the valley; once there he could soon evade pursuit. He bound his rifle securely to him by his belt and crawled out on the shelving rock; then swinging clear by the aid of a tough sapling, he cautiously dropped. He paused to regain his breath, gazing speculatively about him the while. Yes, it was as he had thought. On this side the cliffs broke into a series of giant steps which led easily to the river. "Lucky once more," he chuckled, speaking his thoughts aloud. "That black demon had missed again. Nex' turn is mine, an' I sha'n't miss him."

Thus musing he turned to begin the descent–and faced Judah where he stood in the shadow of a great boulder, with a smile on his face, watching the movements of his enemy the overseer. Thomson turned as if to run down the mountainside.

"Stop where you are!" thundered the giant black.

The man obeyed, but his hand sought his rifle.

"Hands up!" again came the pealing voice. The order was given along the barrel of a gleaming rifle. Thomson's hands went up obediently.

"You are surprised to see me," said Judah grimly. A period of silence ensued. It was a dramatic scene, far from the scene of recent strife. The morning sun had broke in dazzling splendor over the earth; the birds were feeding their young families and flew from tree to tree in neighborly fashion; the murmur of bees humming and of the stream far below mingled harmoniously. All was peace. But within two human hearts surged the wild passions of fierce animals at bay.

Judah looked at his foe with the air of one about entering upon a momentous task. Thomson stood with the narrow ledge for a foothold and the clouds of heaven at his back, facing he knew not what. His head throbbed and in his ears were the drum-beats of an army; his heart was sick with terror for this human torturer, this man-mangler and womanbeater was an arrant coward. When he could bear the silence no longer he spoke:

"I suppose I am your prisoner?"

Judah smiled. It was a terrible smile, and carried in it all the pent-up suffering of two years of bodily torture and a century of lacerated manhood. Thomson feared him, and well he might. Again he spoke. The sound of his own voice gave him courage; anything to break the horrible silence and the chill of that icy smile.

"I am to be treated as a prisoner of war?"

This time Judah answered him.

"Would you have treated me as a prisoner of war if you had captured me?"

"No," broke involuntarily from Thomson's lips.

"Very well!"

"I demand to be taken before Captain Brown. Surely he is human; he will not give me into the hands of a savage to be tortured!" exclaimed the wretch in frantic desperation.

Again Judah smiled his calm, dispassionate smile as he examined his rifle, and then slowly brought it to his shoulder. "You who torture the slave without a thought of mercy, and who could treat a young white man–one of your own race–as you did Mr. Maxwell, fear to be tortured? Why, where is your boasted Southern bravery that has promised so much?"

Bill's teeth glittered in a grin of hate and fear.

"God! It's murder to kill a man with his hands up!" he shrieked.

"It rests with you whether or not I shoot you," replied Judah calmly. "I am going to give you one chance for life. It is a slim one, but more than you would give me."

Bill eyed him with a venomous look of terror and distrust; but his manner had changed to fawning smoothness.

"Judah," he began, "look a-here, I own I done you dirt mean, I do. I ask yer pardon–I couldn't do more'n that ef you was a white man, could I? Well, sir, I know you're a brave nigger, an' I know, too, it's nat'ral for you to lay it up agin me, fer I done yer dirt an' no mistake. But I had to; ef I'd showed you quarter, every nigger on the plantation 'd been hard to handle. It was necessary discipline, boy; nothin' particular agin you."

Bill's beady black eyes never left the Negro's face as he watched for a sign of wavering in the calm smile.

"Look a-here, I can tell you a heap of things 'd be worth more'n my life to the gal, an' Titus couldn't blame me for givin' the scheme away; what's money to life? It's worth a fortune to you to know what I can tell you this minute; only let me out of this, Jude."

But Judah knew his man. Not for one instant did Thomson deceive him. He judged it a righteous duty to condemn him to death.

"You stole Winona's liberty and mine. I know what your promises are worth. Do you think I would listen to a proposition coming from you, you infernal scoundrel? Get ready. I've sworn to kill you and I intend to keep my oath. When I count three jump backwards or I put a bullet into your miserable carcass. If you are alive when you strike the river, you can swim ashore; it's one chance in ten. Choose."

Bill grew white; his eyes gleamed like those of a trapped rat, but he seemed to realize that it was useless to plead for mercy at the hands of the calm, smiling Negro before him.

"One!" counted Judah, moving toward Thomson a step as he counted. There he paused, desiring that the wretch should suffer all, in anticipation, that he had caused others to suffer.

"Two!" Thomson moved backward involuntarily, but still he did not lose his footing. Again Judah paused.

"Three!"

With a wild curse, Thomson sprang off the ledge. A fearfully quiet moment followed. Judah did not move. There came a crashing of underbrush, a sound of rolling rocks and gravel, a plash of water—silence.

(To be continued.)

129

CHAPTER XV.–(Concluded.)

A superb, masterful smile played over the ebon visage of the now solitary figure upon the mountainside. In his face shone a glitter of the untamable torrid ferocity of his tribe not pleasing to see. The first act in his bold and sagacious plans was successful; once free, it only remained for him to carry them out with the same inexorable energy.

The upraised hands and straining eyeballs, rigid and stone-like, the gapping, bloodless lips, the muttered curse–all had passed from sight like an unpleasant dream. Judah, intently listening to the ominous thud, thud, thud, of that falling body, the swish of displaced bushes, and the rattle of gravel and stones, was not moved from the stoicism of his manner, save in the fearful smile that still played over his features. Then, as he listened, there came a last awful cry, a scream that startled all nature and awoke echo after echo along the hillside–a scream like no sound in earth or heaven–unhuman and appalling. He made a step forward to the brink and looked over and then drew back.

A while he leaned upon his gun in meditation. He was a morbid soul preying upon its recollection, without the gift of varied experience; it was not strange that vengeance seemed to him earth's only blessing. To him his recent act was one of simple justice. Hate, impotent hate, had consumed his young heart for two years. An eye for an eye was a doctrine that commended itself more and more to him as he viewed the Negro's condition in life, and beheld the horrors of the system under which he lived.

Judged by the ordinary eye Judah's nature was horrible, but it was the natural outcome or growth of the "system" as practiced upon the black race. He felt neither remorse nor commiseration for the deed just committed. To him it was his only chance of redress for the personal wrongs inflicted upon Winona and himself by the strong, aggressive race holding them in unlawful bondage. Time and place were forgotten as he stood there like a statue. He was back in the past. His thoughts ran backwards in an unbroken train until the scene before him changed to the island and the day when the careless happiness of his free youth was broken by the advent of the strangers, Colonel Titus and Bill Thomson. Then had followed the murder of White Eagle.

Yes, once he had a friend, but he was dead–dead by a man's hand. And he–but a moment since went over the cliff. It was well!

As through a mist, queries and propositions and possibilities took shape, there on the cliffside, that had never before presented themselves to him. As he stood in the blazing sunlight, his brain throbbed intolerably and every pulsation was a shooting pain. Why had he been so dull of comprehension? What if a thought just born in his mind should prove true? O, to be free once more!

There was a rustle of leaves, and out from the shadow of the trees filed a number of anti-slavery men headed by Captain Brown and Parson Steward

"Well, Judah," said Captain Brown, "we've been watching your little drama. You promised to kill him and you've done it."

"Boys," returned Judah, "and all of you, I leave it to you if I'm not right in ridding the world of such a beast as Thomson."

The men set up a cheer that echoed and re-echoed among the hills. The women in the cave heard with joyful hearts.

"I'd kill a snake wherever I f'und him," said one; "wudn't you, Parson?"

"Sure," replied the parson. "This is a holy war, and it's only just begun."

"This is a great day. Praise God from whom all blessings flow; we've put to flight the armies of the Philistines," said Captain Brown.

"It is justice! I am satisfied," said Judah, scanning each solemn face before him with his keen eyes.

Parson Steward wore the same calm, unruffled front touched with faint humor that had characterized him when first introduced to our readers. He was a trifle paler, but that was all that reminded one of the fact that only by a miracle, as it were, he had escaped death at the hands of cruel men. Judah grasped his hand in both of his.

"No wonder we have won, Parson; I heard them cry: 'Look at the Parson!' and then they fled in every direction."

"They reckoned he was dead, an' 'lowed he was a ghost. By gum, how they broke! It was easy work to pick them off," broke in one of the men.

"Perhaps you'll be good enough to tell me where you come from, Parson; you've been dead to us for weeks past."

"Yes; we all want to learn how the Parson got here," said Captain Brown.

"Oh, I been pretty near you right along," replied the Parson, not a whit hurried or excited by the interest of his audience. "That night on the road with young Maxwell was a terrible one. They caught me off my guard for the first time in my life. I was filled with shot and left for dead. Next morning Reynolds got wind of the proceedings and went out to find my remains and give me a decent burial. I was breathing when he got me. That settled it. He toted me on his back to his house and hid me in his loft, and there I lay eight long weeks and every one thinking me dead. Boys, it was a close shave, and when I thought of my wife and children it was tough, turrible tough on the old man, but I left them in the hands of that God who has never failed me yet, and here I am right side up with care, and the old woman and kids safe and hearty here in your camp." He ended solemnly, and the men doffed their ragged hats in humble homage.

"Amen!" said Captain Brown. "All's well that ends well," and they continued their tramp up the mountainside to the cave.

Impelled by a morbid fascination, Judah climbed down the mountain path seeking the bed of the stream below where lay the body of his foe.

CHAPTER XVI

All through the long morning Winona patrolled her beat listening with anxious heart to the sounds of distant firing which the breeze brought to her ears from time to time. At noon one of Captain Brown's daughters brought her coffee; it was the only break in her solitary vigil. She scanned the horizon with anxious eyes, but having no field-glass was unable to distinguish friend from foe among the figures scarcely discernible with the naked eye.

In the dim vistas of the woods it was cool and shady, but the sun beat down mercilessly upon the sides of the cliff, and as she watched the shifting rays she wondered how the battle went in sickening dread, and then rebuked her own impatience for news. As the hours wore on, the shadows began to lengthen; their long fingers crossed the hills pointing darkly toward the river. The girl was unhappy and fearful in her mind; yet she tried to comfort herself, but for a time her firm head played her false enough to picture flames leaping from the woods from the low roofs of the huts amid the corn-stalks, and little children under merciless hoofs, and the awful tumult of flight for life. That was no more than they must expect if the Rangers won. "But they won't win!" she thought, with a brave smile on her face and a heavy heart in her bosom.

Overcome at length by the restless fever within, she determined to risk all in an endeavor to obtain news of her friends–of Warren. She started toward the battle line about the time Judah met Thomson on another spur of the mountain. Reaching the stream Winona followed the bed for some distance in the shadow of the cliff.

Suddenly, far above her head, she heard the gunshot, the scream of agony tearing through space, at once an alarum and rallying cry; it meant to the lonely girl all the savagery of battle; it might mean havoc and despair. She covered her face with her hands a moment, removing them the next instant in time to see a falling body drop into the water almost at her feet. Terror rendered her motionless. The soft waves stole up and flung themselves over the quiet body huddled there breast high in the stream. Then a new thought came to her–"if it should be Warren!" Gathering herself up, she stumbled through the grass to the edge of the river, fell on her knees on the bank and surveyed the helpless shape lying there. A groan broke from the white lips. She nerved herself to move nearer. She took the unconscious head in both hands and turned the face toward herself and–looked into the sightless eyes of Thomson.

Her relief was so great that she sobbed aloud; then after giving broken thanks that it was not Warren, she rose from her knees and began to look about her for means to succor the man before her. He was her enemy, but the mother instinct that dwells in all good women, which can look on death, gave her calmness and strength to do, and the heart to forgive.

She turned to seek help and faced Judah coming out from the trees. "Oh, Judah, he is alive!" she exclaimed, pointing to the inanimate figure in the water. Judah gazed at her in surprise, then said:

"What! Not dead yet? I thought I had settled his case for all time. How came you here?"

"I came out to look for the wounded. Help me to carry this man to camp; surely you are satisfied now. You cannot shoot a dying man," she said, sternly catching the ferocious light that still glimmered in his eyes as he lifted his gun to the hollow of his arm.

"I did it for you as much as for myself. Have you forgotten your father?" he added, reproachfully.

"I do not forget. God forbid! But you have done enough."

"Not enough," replied Judah. "He is the hater of my race. He is of those who enslave both body and soul and damn us with ignorance and vice and take our manhood. I made an oath; it was no idle threat."

He poised his gun. Quick as a flash the girl threw herself before the unconscious Thomson. "You shall not! You make yourself as vile as the vilest of them—our enemies. Let the man die in peace. See, he is almost gone."

"Yes, Judah, it is enough; she is right," said Warren Maxwell's voice as he joined the group by the stream. "Surely you must be sick of bloodshed. Have you not had enough?"

With a glad cry Winona was folded in her lover's arms.

"Let it be as you wish," said Judah after a short time, as he silently viewed the happiness of the lovers. Then he prepared to help Warren lift Thomson from the stream. They turned faint and sick at the sight of the man's wounds. "His back is broken," said Warren, in reply to Winona's questioning eyes.

"It were more merciful to shoot him on the spot," said Judah, but even he felt now the sheer human repulsion from such butchery master him, as they moved slowly and carefully up the steep ascent.

The Rangers were completely routed by the desperate valor of the Brown men. Incredible as it seemed, most of the enemy had been killed outright and a number of prisoners taken, who were to be tried by court-martial and shot, according to the rough justice of the times.

The anti-slavery men met with small loss, but among the wounded was Ebenezer Maybee. With the other wounded men he was carried back to camp; at sunrise the next morning he was aroused form his stupor by a volley of musketry. Steward was at his side. He asked what it meant.

"Well, partner, you know we won the fight," said he. "Captain Brown is a shootin" all the pris'ners; well, now, ain't that tough fer a prefesser?"

"No, not all the prisoners," replied the Parson. "The most of them have been begged off by young Maxwell. He's the most softest hearted young feller I ever met for such a good shot."

"This yer's a good cause to go in, Parson."

The Parson answered grufly, in a choked voice: "You ain't goin' nowhere, partner; we'll pull you through."

Maybee's face worked, and he planted a knowing wink in vacancy. "We've been partners fer a right smart spell, ain't we, Parson?"

The Parson frowned hard to keep back the tears. "You're a man to tie to, Maybee."

"No, now," sputtered Maybee, breaking down at last; "d— ye Parson, don't make a baby er me." Then with a change of voice he asked, "What's come o' Thomson an' the colonel?"

"Devil's got the colonel and he's waiting fer Thomson; we've got him with a broken back next door to this house. Judah did it. My! but that boy's as ferocious as a tiger."

Maybee nodded. "Well, he's a good boy, is Jude; I've knowed him sense he was knee-high to a toad; been through a heap; don' blame him fer bein' ferocious. I ain't sorry I jined the boys, Parson, fer all I got my ticket. It's a good cause, Parson, a good cause, and you'll see a heap o' fun befo' you're through with it; wish't I could he here to see it, too. You found your ol' woman and the kids all safe, Parson?"

"I did," replied the Person, cordially.

"Jes' break it gently to Ma' Jane, partner, that I got my death in an hones' fight, an' tell her she's all right, havin' everything in her name an' power of attorney to boot."

"I will do so," promised the Parson, solemnly.

Winona

One of the men came in with a message for the Parson. Thomson was conscious and going fast; he wanted the Parson and Winona.

Thomson still lived; none knew why; his stupor had left him conscious. Paralyzed in every limb, he could talk in a strong voice and was perfectly sane, and recognized those about him, but he was going fast.

"How long do you give me, doc?" he asked Warren, jokingly.

"Until it touches the heart," replied Warren solemnly.

"Then it will be soon?" Warren nodded.

Thomson appeared to be thinking. "No," he muttered finally with a sigh, "I got to own up. Colonel's dead, ain't he?" Warren bowed.

"Well then, 'taint no use holdin' out. Bring in the gal and Judah, an' take down every word I say if you want the gal to have her own. You're a lawyer, ain't you? Sent out here on the Carlingford case, warn't you? Never struck you that me and the Colonel knew where to find the man you was huntin', did it?" His voice was spent, and Warren, his mind in a tumult, held a glass of liquor to the dying man's lips, and then sent for Winona and Judah and Parson Steward. They came instantly, and with the transient vigor imparted by the liquor Thomson opened his eyes again and said, in a clear tone: "I'm here yet, Judah; I almost got the one chance you offered me, but it ain't for long I'll hender you; I'm goin' fast."

No one answered the wretch, baffled alike in base passion and violent deeds, but Parson Steward began a fervent prayer for the dying. Something of his awful need for such a petition must have filtered through the darkness of the sin-cursed heart and he presently comprehended dimly the great change before him. He whispered at the close:

"That's all right, Parson. I know I deviled you an' tried to kill you; I did the same to the nigger–an' to Maxwell–but I done the girl

138

worse'n dirt. That's me you described in your prayer–a devilish wicked cuss, but I warn't always so, an' d— me ef I ain't sorry! I'm goin' to try to make the damage I've done, good–to the girl, anyhow."

"Miserable sinners, miserable sinners, all of us. Madness is in our hearts while we live, and after that we go to the dead. God forgive us," muttered the Parson, not noting the dying man's profanity.

"Take down every word I say, Mr. Maxwell, an' let me kiss the Book that it's all true."

The scene was intensely dramatic. Winona sat with clasped hands folded on her breast; she knew not what new turn of Fortune's wheel awaited her. Judah's dark, handsome face and stalwart form were in the background where he stood in a group formed by Captain Brown and his sons, who had been called to witness the confession.

As for Warren Maxwell, he felt the most intense excitement he had ever experienced in his life. His hands shook; he could scarcely hold the pen. Most of us creatures of flesh and blood know what that terrible feeling of suspense, of dread, with which we approach a crisis in our fate. It is indefinable, but comes alike strong and weak, bold and timid. Such a crisis Maxwell felt was approaching in the fate of Winona and himself. There in we recognize the mesmeric force which holds mankind in an eternal brotherhood. Stronger than all in life, perhaps, is this mysterious force when a man feels that he has

"Set his life upon a cast,
And must abide the hazard of the die."

"Mr. Maxwell, you came to America to find the lost Captain Henry Carlingford, heir to the great Carlingford estates. You thought you were on a hopeless quest, did you not?" Warren nodded. It was noticeable that the man spoke in well-bred phrases, and had dropped his Southwestern accent. "You found the captain all right, but you never knew it. White Eagle was the man you wanted!"

There was a cry of astonishment from the listeners. Winona was in tears. Into Judah's eyes there crept the old ferocious glitter as he said:

"And so you murdered him! I have suspected as much for two years."

"No, no, Judah; I wasn't in that. Titus did the killing."

Now Warren lost sight of all personal interest in the case, seeing nothing but its legal aspect. He wrote rapidly questioning the man closely.

"Why did Col. Titus commit this murder? How came you to know this?"

With great effort Thomson replied:

"Titus hated him because he stood between him and a vast fortune, and he was also jealous of his wife's love for Henry Carlingford; he was her lover from childhood, and she loved him until death."

"Then if you know this, I want you to tell me who killed young Lord George. Miss Venton was affianced to him. You can tell if you will, for Miss Venton married Colonel Titus." Warren spoke sternly and solmenly.

Thomson muttered to himself and then was silent; all waited breathlessly in painful silence. Would he solve the riddle, and tell the story of the crime for which a guiltless man had been condemned by a jury of his peers years before?

"No, it won't neither," they heard him say, and then he spoke aloud: "Everything must be made clear?"

"Yes," said Warren, "if you wish to help this poor girl whom you have wronged so cruelly."

"It won't be against you when you get on the other side, Thomson. Free your mind, my friend; it'll do you good. Terrible, verily, sir, is the Lord our God, but full of mercy," said Parson Steward.

"I'll take your word for it, Parson, but I never was much on religion; perhaps I'd fared better if I had been. Well, then, I killed Lord George. I swore to bring disgrace upon the entire Carlingford family. And I have done it; I have had a rich revenge. I was Lord George's valet; my sister, Miss Venton's maid. Lord George could never resist a pretty face, and my sister was more than that. Miss Venton loved Captain Henry, and Lord George found her an indifferent woman. She but obeyed her father's orders, and so Lord George made love to the maid, deceived her, and when he tired of his toy abandoned her to the usual fate of such women–the street. I found her when it was too late, and I swore revenge so long as one lived with a drop of the blood in his veins.

"One day the brothers quarrelled bitterly over Miss Venton; then was my chance. I shot Lord George in the back, and fled, knowing that suspicion would fall on Capt. Henry. It did; and two of my enemies were out of my way, for the Captain was tried and convicted and lived an outcast among savages for years; that was my little scheme for getting even. For the sake of his daughter Lillian, Colonel Titus killed White Eagle and held Winona as a slave, thus cutting off the last direct heir to Carlingford."

The faint voice ceased. The narrative was finished with great difficulty; the man failed rapidly. With a great effort he added: "Will you call it square, young fellow?–you and Winona–and Judah? I've done you bad, but I've told the truth at last. Mr. Maxwell–you know the rest–I reckon you'll marry the heiress–I'm glad.–Land in Canidy soon, boys; they'll be after you inside a week–big Government force—." Warren preserved his impassiveness by a struggle; the others followed the faint voice of the dying man with breathless attention; they felt that every word of this important confession was true.

Maxwell was filled with a hope that agitated him almost beyond control.

"Why, surely," he said, at length, in a voice that trembled in spite of himself, as he rose and joined Winona and Judah at the bedside, "I'm awfully grateful to you for telling me this; it makes my work easy."

"I sort o' hated to tell, fer a fac'," he said, falling back into his usual vernacular, "but I'm glad I done it." His voice failed; a gray shadow crept over the white face; all was still.

"Let us pray," and Parson Steward broke the silence. As they knelt about the bed, the crack of rifles broke in upon the fervent petition for mercy sent upwards by the man of God. It was the volley that carried death to the last of the captured Rangers. Guilty soul joined guilty soul in their flight to Eternity.

Ebenezer Maybee expressed no surprise when told of Thomson's confession.

"These happenings 'min' me o' the words o' the Psalmist that I've heard Parson quote so often: 'Thy right hand shall teach thee terrible things.'"

"Amen," said Steward. "But full of mercy, also, since they will deliver this poor girl from the hand of the spoiler."

Many tears were shed over Maybee's precarious condition, for he was dear to every soul in the camp. Winona and Judah established themselves as nurses at his bedside, bringing all their Indian knowledge of medicine to bear upon his case, and declaring that they would pull him through.

"My children," he said, after musing a while on the exciting tale just told him, "I believe I can match that story o' Thomson's. I have a surprisin' secret to unfol' to you. It will make the whole business clear. White Eagle must a perceived his end, an' he says to me, says he, jes' about a month before his disease, he says, 'Maybee, keep this here package if anything comes across me, 'tell my girl's a responsible age.' After he was dead I said to myself–in the words of Scripter, 'a charge to keep I have' an't ain't safe to keep it; so I give the package to Ma' Jane an' she has it unto this day."

CHAPTER XVII

A week later our fugitives started for Canada via Buffalo, N. Y., by a circuitous path well known to Captain Brown. Mr. Maybee went along in an improvised ambulance, much improved in health and bearing well the fatigue of travel.

The Brown camp was deserted, and the Government troops, when they arrive, found only the blackened remains of the once busy settlement. Where the Rangers had paid the penalty of their crimes against the farmers of Kansas, the grass covered the sod as if it had never been disfigured or stained. The last gun had been fired in Kansas by Brown's forces, and he was next heard of in the Virginia insurrection which ended so fatally for the intrepid leader.

After many startling adventures and narrow escapes from capture, a group of bronzed and bearded men and one woman rode up one morning to the entrance of the Grand Island Hotel. It was our friends and the Brown family. The other refugees had passed in safety over the border into Canada, and the fugitive slaves were, at last, rejoicing on free soil.

The front of the hotel was deserted, the women being busy in the rear with their morning duties, and the usual hangers-on not being about.

Mr. Maybee, who was lying on a bed in the bottom of the wagon, sat up as the cavalcade paused, and cried:

"Ma' Jane! Ma'–Jane!"

"Ya'as," screamed a female voice from the rear, not "like a song from afar;" or, if so, it was set in four sharps. "What's up neow?"

To which Maybee, probably reckoning on the magnetic attraction of female curiosity, made no reply, which diplomatic course instantly drew his worthy better half–a big one, too–and far better than her vocal organ. She came followed by the cook, Aunt Vinnie, and 'Tavius. "Law sakes!" she cried, sticking her plump arms akimbo and staring in amazement at the company before her, "if it ain't Ebenezer—an' the Englishman—an' Jude!—an' 'Nona!!" Her astonishment could go no farther. The next instant she had folded the girlish form in her arms in an agony of joy.

"My precious child! Thank heaven we've got you back safe! It's been an awful time fer you."

"Wall, darn my skin!" cried Maybee, wiping his own eyes in sympathy with the weeping woman, "here's me, wounded an' dyin', been a stranger an' a pilgrim in hos-tile parts fer months, an' when I git home the wife of my bosom ain't no eyes fer me nor tears nuther—everybody else is fus'. I call all you boys to witness my treatment; I enter a suit for devorce at once. Ma' Jane, I'm goin' ter leave your bed an' board."

"You ain't no call to be jealous, Maybee, as you well know. Ef you're sick, I'll nuss you; ef you're hungry, I'll feed you."

Then these pilgrims of the dusty roads received a royal welcome from the bewildered woman. Their brown hands were shaken, their torn clothes embraced, their sunburnt faces kissed with a rapture that was amazing.

"Come in, everybody. 'Tavius, git a move on with them hosses and things! Vinnie, stop your grinnin' an' hustle with the dinner."

Mrs. Maybee expanded, metaphorically,—literal expansion would have jammed her in the doorway,—on hospitable cares intent.

'Tavius marched away grinning, while Mrs. Maybee ushered her guests into the house. How long seemed the time to Winona and Judah since they had been torn from that kindly shelter by the slave-hunters; terrible, indeed, had been the times that followed so swiftly.

After the travelers were somewhat rested and refreshed, the story of their adventures was rehearsed, and the stranger one of the wrongs and sorrows of White Eagle and his true name and position in the world was told to an interested crowd of listeners, for the news of Maybee's arrival with Winona and Judah had been industriously circulated by 'Tavius as soon as he could steal away from his duties, and a crowd of leading citizens filled the office, hall and piazza, anxious to see the wanderers and hear the miraculous story of their escape.

"Now, Ma' Jane, you remember the papers I gave you–White Eagle's paper's?"

"Of course,"

"I want you to fetch 'em out and give 'em to the child before us all. Then Mr. Lawyer Maxwell will see ef they is all correc'."

Mrs. Maybee brought a long tin box and placed it in her husband's hand. He opened it. "Let's see. Three legal dockymen's and a few pieces of jewelry. Them's 'em, I reckon. There you are, my girl," he said, tenderly, as he handed the package to Winona. Her attitude was at once tragic and pathetic as she drew back, for one instant, and stood in silent self-repression. A dizziness swept over her. What would the papers reveal? Their contents meant life or death to her hopes. She took the papers without speaking and passed them on to Warren almost mechanically.

"Read them–I cannot."

"Right, child," said Maybee.

There was breathless silence in the room as Warren unfolded the paper lying on top of the packet like a thick letter. All–honor for dead and living, ancient lands and name, home for the fondly loved child–lay sealed in the certificate of marriage and birth lying in Maxwell's right hand. The other papers related to his own story–a record of happenings after the fugitive from justice had arrived in

America. The jewelry was jeweled family portraits, including one of Captain Henry when a young man; also a ring bearing the family crest. Nothing was missing–the chain of evidence was complete, even to the trained eye of the legal critic.

Then followed congratulations and good wishes from the friends who had done so much to make the present joy possible.

"I for one," said the representative to Congress, "from this day out condemn this cursed 'system' of ours. We're a laughing stock for the whole world, to say nothing of the wickedness of the thing."

"Right you are, Jameson; put them sentiments down for every man of us," cried a voice in the crowd.

Judah could say nothing, but he wrung Warren's hand hard.

"You go with us to England, Judah, and share prosperity as you have shared adversity. You shall choose your own path in life and be a man among men."

"I ain't any words to say, my girl!!" Maybee said huskily to Winona; "but you know what's in my ol' heart, I reckon, by what's in your own. I know you won't forget us when you're a great lady. Poor White Eagle, he had a rocky time of it, sure."

* * * * *

Many visits were made to the island by our three friends before the day when they embarked from Canada for old England. Oh the rare delight they felt in the movement of the light canoe as they glided over the blue waters of the lake, and the thunders of Niagara sounded in their ears like a mighty orchestra rejoicing in their joy.

Again they stood on the high ridge where lay the sun-flecked woods, climbed the slopes and listened to the squirrel's shrill, clear chirp; watched the blackbirds winging the air in flight and heard the robin's mellow music gushing from the boughs above their heads.

Winona

The Indian-pipes with their faint pink stems lay concealed among the bushes as of old.

Beneath the great pine that shaded White Eagle's grave they rested reverent, tempered sadness in their hearts. Winona buried her face in her lover's bosom with smothered, passionate sobs. Warren folded her close to him.

"My heart's dearest, you must not grieve; your time of mourning is past. He is happy now as he sees your future assured. Through you he has conquered death and the grave; justice and honor are his after many years of shame." And she was comforted.

They made no plans for the future. What necessity was there of making plans for the future? They knew what the future would be. They loved each other; they would marry sooner or later, after they reached England, with the sanction of her grandfather, old Lord George; that was certain. American caste prejudice could not touch them in their home beyond the sea.

A long story full of deep interest might be written concerning the subsequent fortunes of John Brown and his sons and their trusty followers—a story of hardships, ruined homes and persecutions, and retribution to their persecutors, after all, through the happenings of the Civil War. But with these events we are all familiar. Judah never returned to America. After the news of John Brown's death had aroused the sympathies of all christendom for the slaves, he gave up all thoughts of returning to the land of his birth and entered the service of the Queen. His daring bravery and matchless courage brought its own reward; he was knighted; had honors and wealth heaped upon him, and finally married into one of the best families of the realm.

Winona celebrated in her letters to Mr. Maybee the wonders of her life in England, where all worshipped the last beautiful representative of an ancient family. The premature, crushing experiences of her young girlhood, its shocks and shameful surprises were not without good fruit. She is a noble woman. She is fortified against misfortune now by her deep knowledge of life and its inevitable sorrows, by love. Greater joy than hers, no woman, she believes, has ever known.

* * * * *

At intervals Aunt Vinnie found herself the center of groups of curious neighbors, white and black, who never tired of hearing her tell the story of Winona's strange fortunes. She invariably ended the tale with a short sermon on the fate of her race.

"Glory to God, we's boun' to be free. Dar's dat gal, she's got black blood nuff in her to put her on de block in this fersaken country, but over dar she's a lady with de top crus' of de crus'. Somethin's gwine happen."

An elderly white woman among the visitors drew a long breath, and declared that she had been lifted out of her bed three times the previous night.

"To be course," said Aunt Vinnie. "That's de angelic hos' hoverin' roun' you. Somethin's gwine drap. White folks been ridin' a turrible hoss in this country, an' dat hoss gwine to fro 'em' you hyar me."

"De mule kicked me three times dis mornin' an' he never did dat afore in his life," said a colored brother; "dat means good luck."

"Jestice been settin' on de sprangles ob de sun a long time watchin' dese people how dey cuts der shines; um, um!" continued Vinnie.

"A rabbit run across my path twice comin' through de graveyard las' Sunday. I believe in my soul you're right, Aunt Vinnie," said 'Tavius.

"Course I'm right. Watch de sun an' see how he run; gwine to hear a mighty rumblin' 'mongst de dry bones 'cause jestice gwine plum' de line, an' set de chillun free," and as she retired to the kitchen her voice came back to them, in song:

Winona

"Ole Satan's mad, an' I am glad,
  Send de angels down.
He missed the soul he thought he had,
  O, send dem angels down.
Dis is de year of Jubilee,
  Send dem angels down.
De Lord has come to set us free,
  O, send dem angels down."

THE END.

CPSIA information can be obtained
at www.ICGtesting.com
Printed in the USA
LVOW10s1842010817
543422LV00003B/459/P